Orpheus in Tampa

The Thriller

Russ Stahl

authorHOUSE®

AuthorHouse™
1663 Liberty Drive
Bloomington, IN 47403
www.authorhouse.com
Phone: 1-800-839-8640

First published by AuthorHouse 02/24/2011

ISBN: 978-1-4567-5003-9 (sc)
ISBN: 978-1-4567-5002-2 (ebk)

Printed in the United States of America

Any people depicted in stock imagery provided by Thinkstock are models,
and such images are being used for illustrative purposes only.
Certain stock imagery © Thinkstock.

This book is printed on acid-free paper.

Chapter One

Dantavius Washington fell in love with Joan Barnes when he was 18. He met her at a church dance. She was also 18 and had just moved to Tampa with her mother. They worked at a pharmacy on Fowler-her mother as a pharmacist's assistant; Joan as a certified cosmetologist. Mother and daughter shared an apartment and a small car. Dantavius' parents were together and both worked for the City Water Department. When he turned 18, his father managed to get him a job as a mailman which allowed him to make more than twice what he would have earned in the private sector. He took courses at a junior college –HCC- and hoped to move one day into management at the Post Office. Dantavius and Joan were attractive young adults, full of hope and promise; they met, fell in love and were married six months later in a church wedding with the whole congregation in attendance. Everyone danced with the bride at the reception and commented on her beauty and freshness. She was fresh and virginal. She had insisted that her eager husband wait until their marriage was sanctified by a church wedding.

After the wedding they drove to the beach and honeymooned at the Don Cesar. Everyone welcomed them; they looked like a fashion plate, an advertisement for some exotic island paradise. So ardent were the couple, so unremittingly amorous, that Dantavius thought Joan would surely conceive, but she didn't. In the months that followed, the newlyweds settled into a life of mutual devotion and conjugal bliss. Joan was the practical one, the manager and home economist; she prepared the best meals and furnished the apartment stylishly. They ate out once a week at an Italian restaurant on Dale Mabry and she always paid with cash from her own income.

And then there were the jewels. She had a weakness for them.

You mustn't laugh at me, Dantavius, she said one day, several weeks after the honeymoon. I've always loved rubies and diamonds. I like the way they go together. You know, white and red, like a Valentine. He laughed when he saw her put on the broach; he said everyone would laugh at her. She said she didn't care. She would wear costume jewelry until they could afford the real thing.

It's like magic, he said, beholding the opulent cluster of gems. On you they almost look real.

She wore it everywhere and didn't stop with it but collected a King Solomon's Mine of gaudy treasure.

She worked fewer hours after her marriage and became a perfect wife and housekeeper. He looked forward to coming home from his route and being pampered. She lavished him with attention and favors, feeding and serving him like a king. Despite months of ardor, no fruit sprang forth, no fructification resulted. He wanted to go to a clinic.

She demurred, counseling patience. She said they must let Mother Nature work her magic, but Mother Nature demurred and the months went by. When they went back to the Don Cesar for their anniversary she promised to go with him to a clinic. In a few more months, dear, she said. Let's wait just a few more months.

They bought a new Mustang the next week. She said she hated to ask her mother for help but they would never save the money the way they lived and they could pay it back in small amounts. He had six siblings and got little help from his own parents. It was winter and she loved to drive the car on sunny days with the top down, elegantly dressed and bejeweled, her handsome husband at her side.

It was a blissful spring for them. They decided to start going to HCC together and took up ballroom dancing. One night she appeared in a red gown that took everyone's breath away. He was proud of her when she explained that her mother and she had worked for weeks making the dress.

She was entering on a green light at the intersection of Columbus and Armenia late one afternoon in the month of May when a man in a Hummer ran a red light and ended her life in a horrendous crash. A man at the filling station was sure it was a beige Hummer but was too discombobulated by the loudness of the crash and the screaming of tires to focus on the plates. He said the Hummer knocked the Mustang out of its path, didn't have to change its course, and sped away. The Mustang blocked his field of vision. The police said it was rotated 45 degrees and was facing north on Armenia. The man ran to the crash and found Joan hanging sideways from her seatbelt, dead.

Her death shocked and enraged the Black community, which vowed to find the Hummer. She was remembered in dozens of churches and thousands came to the funeral; their marriage photos appeared on the front page of the Sentinel. Dantavius' supervisor gave him the week off which he spent at his parent's home. He was devastated by Joan's death and said he would never remarry. No one could take Joan's place.

When he moved back to his apartment he felt Joan's absence like a thousandweight of brick. The minister had counseled him about grieving and he had expected to feel miserable and forsaken but wasn't prepared for the crushing depression. He was too dispirited to fix his own meals or go to his parents. He went to a sports bar and watched the games and tried to distract himself. After a month he realized something was wrong. He couldn't pay his bills. His income was inadequate. Joan had earned a small income and her mother had given her a little money; he decided it was her brilliance as a home economist that made their lifestyle possible. He began looking around for a means of paying the bills. The insurance on the car had just paid off the lien. They had no savings. He considered applying to his parents for an emergency loan but remembered their professions of poverty. They were child-poor. He looked with amusement at her faux treasure. There was so much of it, surely it was worth something. He scooped up two handfuls of broaches and necklaces and put them in a velvet sack.

A jeweler on Dale Mabry offered to look at them. Dantavius fished out the diamond and ruby broach and felt like crying and tried to put it back.

Let me see that, please, said the jeweler. It's a very nice

piece. He looked a moment through his loop. Six-thousand, he said, finally.

Dantavius laughed: he thought the man was joking. It's not real, he said.

The ruby is very fine, said the man. I might be able to go higher. What would you say to six thousand five hundred?

Dantavius felt faint, dizzy, he couldn't think. I'll be back, he said, and rushed from the store.

He went to his sports bar and began drinking heavily. He had known it all along but refused to admit it to himself. Her mother hadn't given her the down payment on the car. Not on her salary. They ate like rich people and went through tanks of gas like rich people. So who had shared his wife's favors? He decided to find the man and kill him, but didn't know where to begin.

He went over everything that had happened. What was she doing at the intersection of Columbus and Armenia? It was nowhere near her work. It seemed a good place to start. He drove up and down Columbus and noticed the pawn shops. Perhaps the jewelry had come from one. He decided to be patient and ask questions until he got an answer. He found the busiest, "Big Al" Mizrahis, and parked across the street from it when he got off work. He began noticing a woman in a car leaving every day around 5:30 from the parking lot in the back. After a week he followed her to a lounge on North Armenia called the Chatterbox. He found her at the bar and sat on the next stool. When the bartender asked him for I.D. he said he had forgotten it and left it in his car; could he have a coke? The bartender didn't want to throw him out, said sure, and didn't charge him for the coke because he was a nice-looking young man that reminded him of Barack Obama. The girl was around twenty eight and not attractive. She smiled at him with a smile that needed work. She offered to buy him a drink and he agreed and an hour later she was telling him the story of her life. She had been with "Big Al" Mizrahi for years. She knew the business inside and out. She worked the desk, dealt with customers pawning their VCRs and guitars. She said the boss was bummed over a chic.

A chic? he asked.

A Black chic, she added

His heart sank. It had to be Joan. But why was he disheartened by finding out something he already knew?

So he likes Black chics, he said.

This one. She was so hot. It was like a big tragedy when she died.

How many people knew about them? he asked.

Oh, just Al and me. She did, that's three, but now she's dead.

Do you have a girlfriend? she asked.

No.

Want to come over? We could look at the videos. I don't have all of them. He's still like in mourning over it. I'm sure he'd say, Doris why are you watching stuff that's none of your business? I'm sure he'd be pissed, but he'll never know. I bring 'em back in the morning and put 'em back on the shelf. He's watching the best ones now except that these are good too. I've been getting off on them.

With him doing the chic?

You gotta see. It's more fun if you don't know, like, what happens. Why don't you come over. We could send out for pizza.

He followed her to her apartment which was nearby. She had a junky apartment that smelled like cat waste. He thought he was having a nightmare. He couldn't enjoy the pizza and had to listen to her talk about her ex for an hour —how he had the two kids and she missed them and how one of her cats had just died. Then she lit up a blunt and they began smoking it and she said that the videos were only fun to watch high. You had to "smoke out first". Fifteen minutes later she started relaxing and nestled beside him and turned on her VCR with her remote. He saw his wife coming into Big Al's store and had the feeling it was the first time. The surveillance camera showed her looking at the jewelry case and a monstrously fat and ugly man come out who had to be Al Mizrahi. He made Dantavius think of a merchant in the Arabian nights. He smiled unctuously and took out a tray of jewelry and removed pieces and discussed them. This went on for half an hour, then she followed him to his back office and he showed her more pieces from an open safe. She tried on a string of pearls and Dantavius was sure he recognized it as one he still had-cultured pearls appraised at six hundred dollars. The video ended and another started but was in a bedroom. It was dated the next day, eight months before the wedding. They drank wine and talked and after half an hour Joan stood and began undressing, slowly, seductively. Her glowing back, a warm orange-brown, faced the camera. Dantavius was entranced, transported to their life together. He felt his intense love for her and the man in the video disappeared. Now she was sitting in the man's lap and he was fondling her lovely bosom with fat, bejeweled fingers. Dantavius wanted her back, like Orpheus, he wanted to pursue her into the underworld. Come back, Eurydice, his heart called to her. Now the fat fingers were hanging her graceful neck with glimmering pearls. She smiled a sensual smile, a smile that promised more.

Dantavius knew that the video would not end with intercourse because she had come to the marriage bed a virgin. But how far would she go? She didn't kiss the man. A half hour later she dressed and left and Doris turned off the VCR to get his attention. She had left and returned in tacky red lingerie. The next one is like more of the same, Doris said. I guess she does a little more but I thought maybe you and me could do something. He was elsewhere, consumed with love for his wife, but the girl on the couch knew nothing of this and had her own agenda. She began kissing him. He wanted to see the videos so he would know whether he had to kill the man. He was not going to kill the man because his wife had taken his pearls for nothing. She wasn't married to Dantavius and if she wanted to separate a fool from his money it was not a big deal. He wanted to see all the videos and the only way that would happen was if he started seeing Doris. Maybe she could come over to his place with the videos so he wouldn't have to smell the cats. He planned to ask her. There was no way he could get out of having sex with her so he carried her to bed and tried to have intercourse but he couldn't feel much of anything and he let her give him head. Afterwards, he asked to see more of the videos. She showed the next one on the VCR in her bedroom. It began about the same as the last-drinking and talking in the bedroom. He noted Joan was wearing her pearls. She seemed more relaxed. He thought he could hear her warm musical voice and smell her fragrant flesh. Then she sat in the man's lap and kissed him. Dantavius remembered her kissing him and began crying in his hands. Doris couldn't understand this and wanted to know what was going on-why was he crying?

He said the chic reminded him of an old girlfriend.

She said he had a girlfriend and not to cry. Did he want to do something? They could do anything he wanted.

He said after the video they would do it again but he wanted to watch. She was right. He was getting off on it.

Now the man in the video was undressing Joan excitedly and Joan was kissing his jowly cheeks and running her fingers through his thinning hair. It was clear that an agreement had been struck allowing him greater liberties. She allowed his puffy hands to wander freely, but held herself coyly, to signal that this final liberty was disallowed. He gloated deliriously and Dantavius wondered what this would cost the fool. Didn't he know that he could buy as much on Dale Mabry for fifty dollars. It was called a lap dance. But of course he was expecting more, which Dantavius knew he would not receive – at least until the wedding. He thought of asking the girl to summarize the ensuing videos, but did not trust her as a historian. She was a dope. She was as dopey as they came. All girls knew they had to do exercises after pregnancies. They even had a name for them.

She said the three were the only videos she had. There were about thirty. She didn't dare to take more than three at a time. Dantavius began focusing again when Big Al put diamond earrings on Joan's earlobes. He recognized them and remembered their estimate-two thousand dollars. No wonder she was so excited. He had actually thought of selling them- he had been offered that much by a jeweler- but thought he could get more through the papers selling them himself. Now he didn't want to sell them. He knew that he could liquidate his collection for over sixty thousand but was beginning to appreciate what Joan had to do for it. It was her dowry, which she had brought to the marriage. He respected her for it. Then she was kissing his jowls again and she got up and ran off camera and came back with an armful of lingerie and was putting it on and taking it off.

This is the part I like, said Doris. She is so sexy. I mean I'm so jealous. She has an incredible body. What an ass!

Just like in the magazines. I know why Big Al was in love with her.

How often did he see her?

Almost every week.

Poor Joan, he thought. He was ravished by the sight of her primping and playing in the negligee, naked, dressed, naked, dressed. It aroused him and his new girlfriend noticed and began giving him head and wanted to be mounted. The video ended with Joan dressing and leaving and he had to mount Doris again and wondered at how utterly hopeless she was. He pretended to climax in her so that he could stop and this got her tremendously excited and her skin became clammy. The cat smell and the clammy flesh converged in his mind and he longed to get away. But he wanted copies of the three videos first and she had no blanks so they went to a copy shop and made them. Afterwards she wanted to have a drink and they went to the Tiny Tap off Howard and played Ray Charles, "If You were Mine", and danced and she drank Rolling Rock-her favorite beer.

I'm surprised you like me so much, she said when they sat down. Why's that?

I thought Black guys didn't like skinny chics. This cut him to the quick. No one ever called him Black.

What's wrong?

I hate the Black thing-the idea that I'm different. No one treats me like I'm different.

That's because you're so cute and you talk nice.

Is it?

If you was dark and ugly they would treat you different, but you got this nice thing about you. I knew I would do it.

I like to think of myself as just an American.

If you want, I'll think of you that way. I think I like

really care about you, Dantavius. So I told you you'd get off on the Black chic and you did. You fucked me so good. We can do it again. I mean when we get back.

I have to get up early to go to the Post Office. Can we go out tomorrow night? Maybe I'll take you somewhere.

She smiled and he wished she hadn't.

Bring a couple more of the videos. Don't take any chances. If you don't think its safe only bring one or wait until later. Play it cool.

You're asking me out on a date, she said. I think it's so sweet. And I like the videos too. Especially the other ones. They get so hot. You'll see. I think you'll get really turned on. I can't wait. I better be ready. I gotta feeling tomorrow night things are going to get really wild.

This made him a little sick-imagining what "hot" meant. But he wanted to see all the videos. It was like being with Joan again.

That night he tossed and turned and had trouble sleeping. Then he found himself in the dark, running, running, down a damp, cold tortuous tunnel, deeper and deeper, into the bowels of the earth. He thought this descent would never end and he would run forever downward. Finally he saw a soft, golden glow which grew brighter and the tunnel opened into a grotto and a sunlit sea lapping a brilliant yellow shore. He saw the Don Cesar, coral and majestic, and a woman in a bikini running towards him-Venus emerging from the spindrift, an orange-brown Venus with a smile of love. Dantavius she said, where have you been, dear? Why did you make me wait so long? I don't think we should wait until tonight. The wedding was so beautiful and I've been wanting to all day. I can't wait. I want to make love, dear, please, let's go to our room.

This dream changed everything. Dantavius believed it would recur; he believed his wife had visited him from the other side. He lost interest in killing Mizrahi. In the weeks that followed he watched all the videos with Doris. He wanted to appreciate what his wife had done for him. He saw Mizrahi as a pathetic slob, and came to feel sorry for him. But something interested him-it might not mean anything, but it might mean a great deal. The videos became increasingly pornographic and ended three months before her death. Why did they end? Doris remembered that she stopped coming when Mizrahi left town. He went to New Jersey to visit his sick mother-his dying mother. She thought this might be related to the termination of the videos.

Chapter Two

Dantavius got a letter from a law office that asked him to call for an appointment. The letterhead indicated that the law firm was in the Monroe Bank Building, a prestigious address and one of the biggest skyscrapers in town. The three man firm specialized in probate law. He looked up the term. It involved wills, trust, inheritances. Joan didn't have a will. He made an appointment for the next day and found himself in the office of the senior partner, Brian Maxwell, a sixty year old silver-haired gentlemen, who offered him coffee and chatted with him a few minutes about how much the tragedy had upset everyone and how they were still looking for the hit-and-run driver. Then he asked Dantavius if he knew about Joan's will. Dantavius said he didn't know Joan had one. Maxwell said that Joan had an estate of half a million dollars; actually somewhat more. She had named her mother the beneficiary of an insurance policy which was not included in the estate. Dantavius didn't seem to understand at first: he sat open-mouthed. Your wife seems to have received some very sapient advice in securities investment. Most of the estate is in IBM shares, which as everyone knows, have been doing well.

Mr. Maxwell, Dantavius said. Where did this come from?

I assumed you knew.

I didn't know anything. I didn't know she had a will.

You knew nothing?

No.

Yes, I see. Well, I'm afraid I can't help you there. Mrs. Washington retained us to draft her will but that was the extent of our involvement. You will of course need to probate the will. We will be happy to do this for you. Probate will allow the securities to be transferred to you. My partners and I have decided that in view of the enormity of this matter we want to handle the probate gratis.

Without charge?

Yes, it will be our pleasure. It should be a fairly simple matter. Mrs. Barnes, her mother, has indicated she won't contest the will. She was also very surprised about the inheritance.

That's really nice of you, Dantavius stammered after a moment.

Mr. Maxwell, are you sure you don't have any idea where this money came from? Dantavius thought the lawyer averted his gaze before answering.

None. Truly. Then he paused dramatically. Mr. Washington, all of us enjoyed your wife's visits. She had a winning way about her. She was so natural, so warm and engaging. We all loved her. She was of course an extraordinarily beautiful woman and she had a wonderful inner quality.

Chapter Three

Mizrahi had not given her half a million dollars. She was a courtesan. He had thirty videos to attest to it. But there was something more; something he didn't know anything about. He ordered drinks for everyone at his sports bar but told no one of his inheritance. He had a couple beers and began to relax and thought how foolish it was to assume one knew anything about anyone.

Then he remembered the accident report. There had been no skid marks from the Hummer. What did it mean? It meant he didn't try to slow down. He had immediately resumed his course. A drunk wouldn't have the presence of mind to do that. Not ordinarily. He didn't want to slow down because he wanted to kill her. He sped away because he didn't want to get caught. Did Mizrahi kill her? He thought of the fool trying to mount her from behind and failing. He thought of the videos as comical. He wondered how much of the five-hundred thousand had come from "Big Al". His intuition told him that little or none had and that "Big Al" was not a killer. What had happened in the three months before her death?

Chapter Four

The next day he went to Joan's mother, an attractive forty-two year woman who lived alone in an apartment in North Tampa. He discussed his reason for thinking the Hummer had been used to kill Joan and told her everything about Mizrahi. She did not seem surprised.

Dantavius, you're just looking for trouble, my dear. You must let this go. I knew, of course I did. She gave me thousands. That's how I bought my new car. You are so kind to understand. She did it for you as much as herself. She loved you. Yes, there was a lot of money. She must have spent fifty thousand on clothes in Tampa. Of course you're not aware of these things.

I noticed she had a lot shoes, he said. And sure, she always had beautiful clothes. But Big Al didn't give her all of it. It sounds like she collected a million dollars since she got to town.

Oh, I didn't think it was that much but it was certainly a great deal and you may be right. A million? Yes. It's possible.

Were there others? he asked.

Yes, of course there were others. She talked about Big Al. He gave her jewelry and you know how she loved jewelry.

Did she mention any of these other men?

Perhaps. Yes, yes…… but why can't we forget this?

Because someone killed her and I don't want them to get away with it.

You want them to kill you too? Dantavius, let it go. There's nothing that can be done. Things like this happen here and nothing's done about it. You know that. Maybe she was murdered. I had this thought, of course I did, but we are powerless little people. We must be grateful they didn't kill us. I know that sounds horrible, dear, but that's just the way things are. You need to forget this and let yourself heal.

Who else?

Who else? Oh, my, let me think. No one that would kill her. Very wealthy men. When she said she was going somewhere with me she almost never was. All the long weekends and evenings. She was with them . But they were older men. Stable men. Dear, this is a waste of time. It won't lead anywhere.

She must have told you their names?

Yes, but this is a mistake my dear. I don't want you to do this. You simply mustn't. You're so young. You don't understand what's at stake here. You mustn't do anything to embarrass these men.

You won't tell me their names?

No, no, no. It's a mistake.

Was she fighting with any of them?

No. They adored her. Well, you would know. Now you want to embarrass them? I simply can't let you do this, dear.

I figured out she left Mizrahi.

Oh, I didn't know.

He could tell by her expression she was lying.

But all these rich guys were happy and seeing her when she died and had no reason to kill her?

Oh, no. She saw them regularly, each one, right up to the end.

And they knew about the others?

Oh yes. That's how it all began. With one. Then he introduced her to another. They're all friends and were older men who adored her.

He wondered if Maxwell was one of them. He imagined her going to him about a will and his finding out that she was married and Mizrahi was giving her money. "Big Al's" photo was in the yellow pages. If she would dispense favors to "Big Al" it was safe to assume that she would dispense them to anyone. He sensed that Maxwell had lied to him when he said he didn't know where she got the money.

Dantavius went away from the visit believing that Joan's mother knew more than she was saying about Joan's death. He thought he understood why Joan had done it. She loved him and the sex act with them meant nothing to her. In the videos she was acting, every gesture was an act. She was somewhere else. It was demeaning to be sure but she was earning more than a million a year. She was a highly paid actress who had worked for him.

Now he was 20 and rich and she was dead. Murdered. He should go on his way, said her mother. Dantavius sensed that she had a reason for wanting this. She was still a beautiful woman; for the men, the clientele, might not she have something to offer? Wouldn't she have stumbled onto at least one opportunity? She was well-disposed to the clients. And protective.

He sat drinking beer in his apartment and looking at

Joan's portrait-his Eurydice. Perhaps it was something that had nothing to do with sex. He had a hunch that it had all happened in the three months after the videos stopped. Mizrahi had mourned her. Would he have mourned her after killing her? Why would these men, any of them, have killed her? He had only been with three other girls but he thought he appreciated her uniqueness. He never looked at another girl after meeting her. She had tortured him for six months, sinking the hook, then immersed him in affection.

He could not imagine a paramour killing her; they must have all been in love with her. Maybe it "was" "Big Al", kicked to the curb for more distinguished and wealthy men.

Chapter Five

After seeing all the videos, Dantavius tried to stop seeing Doris, but that proved impossible. She kept coming over and when he tried to lock her out she threatened to kill herself. He resigned himself to the relationship and decided to make the best of it. He gave her money to have her teeth worked on and bought her an exercycle. He encouraged her to eat more and she gained and looked better and began wearing some of Joan's clothes. He went from not being able to stand her to tolerating her. She became a sort of full time maid and helpmate. She thought of herself as a wife.

She was going through Joan's purses when she found a baggage ticket from Caribair in an envelope. Inside was a notation, "Royal Leeds" with a twelve digit number. Dantavius got on his computer and found out it was a bank with branches all over the islands. How could he find out where the baggage went and when? He called Caribair and they told him –to Cayman Islands on the first Friday of March, Mrs. Jarvis Wilson had flown there for the weekend, returning on a Sunday.

Dantavius realized that he was no longer interested in delivering the mail, called in sick and said his absence would be indefinite. He flew to Cayman Islands the next day and checked into the Cayman Tradewinds. He had made an appointment on line to see a lawyer and took a cab to the main drag, with its big English banks and its office buildings. He noticed the Royal Leeds. The lawyer reminded him of an uncle, an ingratiating 40 year old, light-skinned Black. Dantavius told him that his married sister had asked him to make a withdrawal from a numbered account. How could he do this? That was easy, said the lawyer-McMahan. All he needed was a letter from the sister with a correct signature and of course the number. Dantavius typed a short note authorizing him to withdraw fifty thousand dollars from the account. He signed Joan Wilson with Joan's handwriting and went the next afternoon dressed in a blue suit. He carried a briefcase. He thought he would not mention the letter. A young woman took him to see a man in an office. The man was very cordial and said that Mrs. Wilson did have a lockbox with that number and she had also given her maiden name, Washington. He gave Dantavius the key to the lockbox and opened the gate to a large vault lined on both sides with lock boxes. Anyone with the number had access to the lockbox and full access to the client's records. Dantavius's hand trembled as he unlocked the box. It loosened a lid. He lifted this lid and pulled out the box. It was over a foot long. It had a lid: he lifted the lid and saw hundreds in bundles, it was full of them. He got dizzy and couldn't think, then he dug out a few bundles and tried to estimate the amount. Each bundle contained a hundred bills and was denoted Ten Thousand. In a few minutes he counted a million and change. He put them all in his briefcase and closed the box with shaking hands, then left the bank and walked four blocks to a Swiss bank called Eurobank and went inside. He asked for a numbered account and deposited all but two hundred thousand in it. He memorized the number before he left the bank.

When he got back to his room he collapsed on his bed. His nerves were shot. Nervous exhaustion, he thought. What does it mean? Joan was involved in sex. Could men pay that much for sex? He didn't think it was possible. What was she doing on trips? He remembered the clerk at Royal Leeds saying that all her account information was available to him. That suggested to him that she might have an account there in addition to the numbered one.

He went the next morning and said his sister wanted him to get her balance. He was sitting in the man's office again. He got on his computer and Dantavius saw figures come up on his screen.

Yes, she has a small account here, said the clerk. There it is. Six thousand and twenty three dollars. I'm afraid I can't tell you about these other accounts because they're not here. No, here's one I can access-almost a million. It's in Guernsey. These numbered accounts usually pay rather poor interest. Now here's something interesting- a securities account right here in Grand Cayman-a fair amount of IBM- a couple hundred thousand I should think. It's really gone up hasn't it? And she has some Home Depot. That was smart. It had to come back didn't it? She's got the best stock here….it shows a four percent gain this year. She'll be happy about that. How is your sister….we haven't heard from her.

I'll be representing her interests, said Dantavius, weakly. She's not well.

I'm sorry. You favor her. She made quite an impression

here you know. Give her our best please and our prayers for a speedy recovery. A total here on the stock, eight hundred and four thousand. Merritt and Capp is the securities brokerage. They're in the Dorchester Tower just down the street. You might want to look in on them.

Dantavius's head was spinning. He realized that he was out of his depth. He needed to see a probate lawyer in Grand Cayman and call Maxwell. But could he trust Maxwell? He went to his hotel, dressed in swimming trunks and walked to the beach.

Balmy day, sea breeze in the palms, a crystalline robin's egg sky. He looked out over the water with its greens and blues alternating to the seamless horizon and white sailboats scintillant in the joyful Caribbean sun. He was free, tan, almost 21, and rich. He looked about and felt like he had come home; everyone looked like him; he was in Barack Obama Land.

Chapter Six

Dantavius swam and drank pina colada's from fresh ingredients and enjoyed the girls in string bikinis. After a few drinks he began thinking. Sometimes you have to relax to think. At first he became mildly disturbed and tried to grasp just what it was that was disturbing him. It had to do with all the wealth and where it had come from. Apparently, she had more in other countries . This bothered him deeply because there had to be a reason. Then the sand burst with a plume of dust beside his beach chair, about six feet beyond it, and he heard the crack of a rifle and rolled off his chair and raced into the surf and dove. The entire maneuver didn't take two seconds and another shot rang out before he was under the shallow water swimming frantically. He had the prescience to alter his course so the shooter would not spot him when he came up for air. He did this gingerly, with his face breaking the water to gasp a single mouthful before he continued, well below the surface.

As soon as he got a hundred feet offshore he began swimming parallel to the beach. No more shots. He stood up, felt the sandy bottom and took a peek. Another 100 feet down the beach a party of natives were sunbathing and playing volleyball. He saw no one with a gun. Beyond the party, the beach got gradually more crowded. He swam towards the spot, stood up and ran into the crowd. No shots. In the area where the shots had been fired, three police-Blacks in white British uniforms and pith helmets-were running down to the water. They had heard the shots. Surely this would discourage the shooter.

Dantavius ran to the lawyer's office 15 minutes away and ran up the stairs, not waiting for the elevator. He was a little out of breath when he opened the hall door and strode into the waiting room. The receptionist recognized him and got Mr. McMahon, who appeared and led him into his office. Dantavius related what had happened.

Why wasn't he winded? asked McMahon.

He ran relays on the high school track team. Dantavius recounted the shooting. Yes, it's related to the millions, said McMahan, after a moment. It has to be.

Why is there so much? asked Dantavius.

It's hers, yes, McMahon ruminated. How did this happen? How did she get it?

Fraud? asked Dantavius.

Alright. That's an idea. But a cosmetologist defrauding someone on this scale? Impossible. She did something to get it. What did she do? But this is the least of our problems now. We've got to get you somewhere safe. I can't let you go to the airport. They could be waiting. But why do they want to kill you?

They know from Royal Leeds that I know where the money is and will try to inherit it.

Yes, I can see that. I have a plane. It's a few hours to Veracruz. I could drop you there and let you take a connecting flight to Mexico City. I have a good friend there-a Mexican lawyer. He will help you establish a new identity and disappear. That shouldn't be hard in a city of twenty million.

I have two hundred thousand in a briefcase in the hotel safe, said Dantavius .

We can't go near the hotel now. I'll lend you a few grand until you get Mexico City and can have money wired to a bank. He took Dantavius to his house and gave him some clothes and money and an hour later they were getting into a small two engine plane. Three hours later they landed at a small private airport in Veracruz. Dantavius decided to take a bus with the peasants to Mexico City. McMahon agreed to represent his interests in Grand Cayman. The first thing he intended to do was set up an estate for his wife and try to freeze the funds in the various worldwide accounts. He felt he would have no trouble getting the money at the stock brokerage.

He knew them. But that was not the first order of business-it was to safeguard Dantavius.

Dantavius took a cab to the bus station and was put off by the squalor-the stench of it, the reek of urine. It was night, around eight o'clock. He ended up paying the cab one hundred dollars to drive him to Mexico City. This took five hours and appalled Dantavius. He had never been to the Third World. The unmitigated squalor; a world of shanties and half naked urchins running in the streets, sometimes in groups; even the chickens looked half-starved. The population had a stunted look-undersized men, leathern gnomes under five feet, beggar women with filthy children on every corner, the wretched stench which smelled to him like urine and rotten mangos. He had his driver take him to a huge hotel, gracious and colonial, and called Menendez, the Mexican lawyer. He got a recording in Spanish. He had taken it in high school but he couldn't understand it. He thought no one learned a foreign language in an American High School. He left a message referencing McMahon.

The next morning he learned that his driver had taken him to the Zona Rosa, the Pink Zone, an upscale commercial district-streets of international stores. He went to the Bank of Mexico and decided against it once he got inside-a gigantic 19th century building. It occurred to him that it might not protect the privacy of his account. He needed to talk to the lawyer. He was anxious about having his money in Cayman. He wanted it wired to a Mexican bank. When Menendez didn't answer his phone he called McMahon and learned from the receptionist that there had been an accident. Someone had run into McMahon's car in an intersection and killed him. Nothing was known about the hit and run. Dantavius tried to talk to McMahon's partner but the man was afraid to talk to him. They work fast, thought Dantavius. He called his hotel in Cayman and said he was wiring money to hold his hotel room for a couple weeks. Late on the night of the second day Menendez returned his call. He knew what had happened to McMahon and was not especially eager to meet with Dantavius. He gave him the name of a high-powered attorney whose offices were in the Zona Rosa. David Gutierez. He said he was trustworthy but very expensive. Dantavius met with him the next morning. He had been a federal judge and was in his sixties; he made a favorable impression on Dantavius. Gutierez agreed to take care of everything. He said recovering the money would involve international tribunals but that he would be very surprised if any claimants came forward.

Your wife was involved with some heavyweights. She was not holding these assets for anyone else. I don't believe this. She had been paid for doing something. We don't know what it was but we know great sums were involved and there were winners and losers. We don't know what is involved here but once we dig into it and begin making claims we will find out.

How will we do this?

I will set up an estate here in Ciudad de Mexico and make claims on the accounts through these international bodies. If no one comes forward to deny your claim that you are inheriting from your wife and she is Wilson, the tribunals will award the funds to you.

I'm sure she didn't pay income tax on the money. Can I get in trouble for that?

Oh, no. It will be for the U.S. Government to assert tax liens and you will be making these claims as a Mexican citizen. Con su permisso, with your permission, I will make you one. I will also give you a legal name change. It's unlikely the U.S. will become involved or try to come to Mexico to impose a lien. So you want to find your wife's killer. I've got a better idea-how about just trying to stay alive? Let me worry about getting the money. I feel so good about this I'll agree to a ten per cent contingency as my fee. Your money will be wired to Banco de la Fronterra. Go there tomorrow afternoon. Ask for Senor Lopez. They'll be expecting you. You will stay in this hotel. El Asturiano; its not far. You will stay as Carlos Cintron. Charley Lemon. I am most intrigued by this caso misterioso. Dress as a Mexican. You are a gentleman of color. You will fit in. We have many mulatos here. Dress as a young Mexican of means. So you can speak Spanish?

Two years in high school.

Then you will learn quickly. Here is a cell phone number where you can always reach me. I will obtain your cash from the hotel in Cayman and your papers and try to have her securities transferred to your name. I should be able to do this in a week, after I have obtained an order from the Mexican probate court directing the Cayman firm to do this. You have your marriage certificate and your wife's death certificate at the hotel. This is all I need. With a Mexican court order I see no problem.

How long will it take you to obtain Mexican citizenship for me?

I will do that tomorrow. Here is a cell. Keep it on you at all times so that I can contact you.

The next afternoon Dantavius went to the bank and waited three hours while the money was wired. He kept the money in dollars and withdrew five thousand dollars worth of Mexican pesos, a staggering amount of pesos. He spent the rest of the day shopping for Mexican clothes and emerged from a couturier looking like Carlos Limon. His hair was frizzled and black. He went to a barber and had it straightened and dyed dark brown. Then he decided he never liked looking Black and now it could cost him his life. He asked around and found the best plastic surgeon in town. He said he wanted to look Latin and not Black. The doctor was aghast and said this was a mistake, he was a handsome young man. His nose wasn't too thick and it was the only thing that gave away his Black ancestry- the thick nose with the flared nostrils. Make it more Spanish, said Dantavius.

It will alter your entire appearance.

This is what I want.

The next day the doctor performed a rhinoplasty and a few days later removed the dressings and voila, Dantavius was gone; he had become Carlos Limon. He went to the Gutierrez's office a week later; it had all but healed by then.

Gutierrez said he couldn't believe his eyes-he had become someone else. So he wanted to live after all.

Let's not worry about solving any crimes or righting any wrongs. These people are savages and they want you dead. By the way, I have some good news. I have the probate orders and an agreement in the offing on the securities. I'm paying a few bucks to someone at Merrill-Capp, to grease the wheels, to make them turn faster. We'll have the securities soon and you can pay me a fee. I didn't take my fee on the money I recovered from the hotel safe. Your stock is worth over a million now, Carlos. I hope you don't mind me calling you that. I think you should get used to it. Here are your ID papers by the way. Senor Limon. Charley Lemon. I thought that was a nice touch.

Chapter Seven

Carlos tried to get used to the idea of shedding his past and living the rest of his life as Charley Lemon. He immersed himself in Spanish. He moved into the most exclusive residential tower in the city, into a penthouse, which he had decorated in Latin American ultra chic. But he couldn't accept that his wife had been murdered and the culprits would escape. He imagined them sharing new delicacies- the older men who adored her. Someone didn't adore her. Or McMahon. And what in the hell were they up to? And where did the millions come from? This piqued him.

Gutierez introduced him to his nephew, Hugo Mann, a handsome, blonde-haired, blue-eyed 28 year old playboy abogado (lawyer) in his firm. He met Carlos after his metamorphosis and he had never heard of Dantavius Washington. He took Carlos everywhere. Carlos was a magnet for girls. He looked seventeen, like a high school track star. He had kept in shape jogging and delivering the mail. They were sitting in the lounge of a hotel with a hundred and fifty year old oak bar with huge mirrors and

Mexican tile on the floor surrounded by potted ferns and luxuriant tropical flowers. Hugo loved speaking English and delighted in speaking a literary high-toned English. He sounded to Carlos like an aristocrat in a 19th century novel.

Do not get the idea, my friend, that I am a libertine who wants to make love to every beautiful woman in town.

Carlos laughed. He had seen him with three different girls in a month.

Don't laugh. It's true. I am a connoisseur. You don't know German?

No.

You must learn it. The ancient language from which all others spring. Aryan. That's what we are, my friend. Visigoths. Germans. In German, a connoisseur is a Feinschmecker. Fein means fine, of course and schmecker-smacker would be the English cognate, a taster or sampler. I am a Feinschmecker. Ich bin ein Feinschmecker.

Sampling girls?

Yes, but only the finest.

So, Hugo thinks I'm a Spaniard of pure blood, a descendant of the Visigoths. Carlos smiled at the thought of how he had become a German with a suntan. He had gotten lighter as a result of not being outdoors. He knew that Whites did not know that Blacks also became darker from sunlight and lost their tans just as easily.

So what's wrong with you, Carlos? asked Hugo. Why don't you start dating girls? You've had ten opportunities.

My wife died recently. I think she was murdered.

Really. Who killed her?

I have a hunch but what I need to find out is why. I think that would interest the authorities.

Not here in Mexico, said Hugo. Not anywhere. They're mostly interested in collecting their paychecks. In Mexico they don't do more than they have to and I think this is universal. So why do you think they killed her?

That's what so amazing, said Carlos. This is embarrassing.

Not among friends, said Hugo.

Well, she's dead, of course, said Carlos. But I'm still embarrassed. I think she was, no, I know she was a courtesan. She kept it a secret from me. Someone gave her a huge fortune-millions.

That explains your affluence, your penthouse.

Yes. But I don't think they killed her because of sex. It doesn't make any sense.

Why not?

Her clients were rich old guys who shared her. I thought maybe one of them killed her because she dropped him, but he didn't have the resources to explain her millions or hiring a hit in Grand Cayman. So I'm out theories. It kills me that they're getting away with it and that I have no idea what it's all about – the reason for her death.

You've got to turn your lights on. You don't know how to think. You never studied logic, I'll bet.

No.

Well, it's like having intelligence and not learning how to use it. Logic is essential. You could know the answer now.

How could I?

By failing to consider something.

Carlos thought of how he had never gone through his wife's clothes and how Doris had found the contents of his wife's purse and this had led to what followed- his becoming wealthy. So what else had he missed?

You must appreciate that we are a race of supermen, said Hugo.

We Aryans? said Carlos, laughing. We Visigoths.

35

Yes, why do you laugh? The Spanish Visigoths went on to perform great prodigies after their defeat by Islam. The re-conquest of Spain, La Reconquista, El Cid. Then the conquest of the New World. You are a conquistador and you must act like one.

Carlos laughed and couldn't stop.

Don't laugh, stop laughing. It's true. Cortes, with a few thousand men, came, saw and conquered vast Mexico. And it's still ours. Go to any city in Mexico; go into the biggest bank and ask to see the president of the bank. It will be a White Man. These little brown Indians do nothing but procreate and subsist on corn.

What seems to be their problem?, asked Carlos, still laughing.

They are uncompetitive; they can't produce wealth.

Alright.

You say alright, but you don't understand. You're lights are not turned on. It is true. We are a race of supermen.

Stop it Hugo. You're cracking me up.

No. Our cousins in Germany are literally the most competitive people in the world. They have no resources but sell three times as much per capita as the sorry Americans.

Sorry? Why sorry?

Because of the untermenschen.

The what?

You must learn German. I will give you a book, "under men", sub humans. Well, lets say "the inferior ones", humans, but below us.

Like me, thought Carlos.

So you think I have the answer, but don't know it? said Carlos, changing the subject.

You may. You must think. That is all I do at the firm. I don't spend ten hours a week at the office, but I'm always thinking. People work, work, when they should be thinking. They don't know what the question is most of the time.

What is the question? asked Carlos. He smiled at the thought that like many Blacks, like Michael Jackson, he had always wanted to be White. Now, he had become White with a simple surgical procedure and had a friend who really liked being White. Hugo, the Visigoth, the logician, the superman. Maybe Hugo could help him figure things out.

The question, said Hugo, is which of these girls are we going to make love to?

No!

I like those two sitting against the wall.

Two doe-eyed beauties in their mid-twenties, quintessential Latin Madonna's, with voluptuous figures; they looked a little overripe to Carlos. They could have been ten years older than he.

Are you sure they're Aryan enough?

For our purposes, yes.

I don't know.

You're not thinking like a Conquistador. You must become a Conquistador and a thinker. I'm going to help in this.

Carlos followed him over to the girls, who were delighted to have them sit at their table and pickup the tab. Hugo's reputation proceeded him. The girls knew several girls who had dated and succumbed to him and knew him for what he was- a Don Juan, a hit and run artist. Carlos intrigued them, he was misterioso. He was dressed elegantly and looked like an athlete. He couldn't understand their rapid, jocund Spanish. They were shamelessly coquettish, they used their bright eyes and flashing teeth like an angler uses his lure. Carlos thought that Hugo had out-smarted himself, that he would be happier with a wife and child than pursuing one prey after another. The girls played hard to get, said no to dinner and nightclubbing. Tomorrow was Sunday and they wanted to go to the bullfights. Why didn't the two men take them?

Carlos had no interest in getting involved with the girls. They were too old for him and not to his taste. He didn't want to get involved because of Joan. He wanted to keep her constantly in his thoughts and find her killer. He believed that Hugo could teach him to think. He had almost died in Cayman because he had not thought fast enough. In retrospect he saw he had acted recklessly. He should have known he was in danger.

He got a call the next morning and met Hugo at his lavish condo. The girls were there drinking coffee. They looked even older in the lighting, but they were very beautiful women. The smaller, Clarita, gravitated towards him. This had been decided before he arrived. She talked English to him; maybe she was the one who could talk English better. He told her to talk Spanish. But please talk slower. She said Mexicans couldn't talk slow. They were always laughing and it cheered him up and he decided that maybe it wasn't such a bad idea-going to the Bullfight with Mexican girls. They seemed to get more beautiful and desirable by the minute.

Carlos was awed by the spectacle of the bullfight-the matador marching in like a prince with his retinue, all in 18th century costumes of the same color with white stockings. A band blared traditional music, clarion, brassy. It would break out again at stages in the fight. Then a moment of anticipation and the explosion of the bull into the ring. It stampeded over the packed yellow clay and circled the ring, black, enormous, horns high and proud. The fight itself was anti-climatic. The bull charged a horse and gored a mattress strapped to its side while it took a long spear in its hump from the rider. Hugo explained that at one time there had been no mattress and the horse always died. Then the bull confronted the matador who shook his red cape, or muleta, to provoke the bull and the bull made its first charge. The matador turned with the bull, which trotted aimlessly a moment, then stopped and turned and began regarding the bullfighter and charged the cape again. This was repeated a few times; then the matador, withdrew a pic from his cape and implanted it in the bull's hump as it passed.

This was repeated on the next pass with a second pic. Hugo explained that the pics weakened the bull and made it difficult for the bull to raise its head. Now a picador on foot was implanting two pics at once in the diminished bull and the matador implanted his third and last pic, and with great drama, drew his sword from his cape. He easily dispatched the bull with it and the beast fell to its knees and collapsed on its side.

In the next fight, the matador and his men were in blue instead of green but the fight was in all other ways identical. Carlos saw it as the ritualized slaughter of a dumb brute that did not have the resources to deviate one wit from the plan: the passes became monotonous- a lugubrious, pointless slaughter which ended with the beast yielding to the sword and falling to its knees, then collapsing, stiff-legged, and the ignominious dragging of the carcass around the arena by two mules and out the bull ring to the butcher. Carlos felt he had seen enough for a lifetime and couldn't understand why anyone went to bullfights.

Hugo sensed his ennui and assured him that third fight would be better. The girls were getting attention- the cynosure of a hundred eyes. He realized why they were there-to bask. They drank red wine from a skin bladder and Carlos tried to surrender himself to the moment.

When the band announced the next bull fight the crowd fell silent and a party in gold costumes made their procession into the bull ring. The bullfighter was in his fifties; he looked to Carlos like a troll-squat, grotesque, a little bowlegged.

This is why we came, said Hugo. It's El Moro, the best matador in Mexico, I think our best ever, and of course, the bull. The crowd was excited; everything was different, as if transported to a different time and place. The bull exploded into the arena and looked like a king striding around the ring. Where the others had looked about aimlessly, he communicated his fury with a straight-ahead gaze. The horse trotted out and the bull moved towards it slowly, gored it and jolted it. With a spear in its hump the bull pressed the horse until its horns penetrated the mattress and the horse stumbled to its knees and onto its side, throwing the picador. The crowd was exultant, celebrating death. Then the bull stood in the middle of the ring, regarding El Moro; its body frozen. This moment lasted an eternity. When it came the charge was furious, thunderous; El Moro held the cape close to his body, as if inviting death; when the bull passed the man was miraculously spared. The crowd cheered. With one voice it called the bull's name-Gigante. Hugo shouted to Carlos that it had killed a picador in Guadalajara and survived a fight. It was a legend. Carlos noticed that its horns were larger than the earlier bulls and the animal itself looked bigger. He imagined it strutting from the ring after its successful fight, with colorful pics flapping from its hump and the protruding sword.

There were two more thunderous charges and El Moro

withdrew a pic theatrically and regarded the bull. It froze a moment then began tossing the saliva from its muzzle, lowered its head and pawed the clay with one leg and snorted. Everyone knew something would happen. There was a silence and a pause that went back to the beginning of time. Then the bull charged and El Moro stood his ground, erect and graceful, holding the cape close and prepared to turn, as the bull took the cape, but there was a jagged alteration in the bull's movement and El Moro was in the air above the bull's horns, turning in the air, then rolling on the ground. The bull stopped its forward charge and scrambled back to the body then, as if rooting with its horns, tossed the man several feet ahead; like a rag doll, it flopped to earth.

Now clowns were flitting about the beast and a horse and rider were trying to spear it and it threw its head from side to side, disoriented by the confusion. The crowd was on its feet chanting. Gigante! Gigante! El Moro refused to die. He lost consciousness momentarily when he hit the ground the first time, but was now reviving and dragging himself over the yellow clay with a trail of blood. El Moro was no longer a man; he had become will. He was crawling to his sword which was in the muleta, which lay torn and stained with blood. The bull charged a clown who ran straight for the wall and scampered over it. Then the bull began strutting, looking from side to side, as if assessing things. It saw more clowns imploring the matador to come with them and was distracted by one who ran at the bull, then ran for the wall. Now El Moro was standing up holding his tattered cape, propped up on his sword, and the bull was frozen, regarding him with head raised. The bull and El Moro wanted the same thing. The bull lowered its horns, charged the tattered cape and swept El Moro off his feet with a brush of its legs bearing the cape off on its horns. It slowed to a stop, confused by the red flannel in its eyes. El Moro stood up slowly and propped himself on his sword and waited for death. The bull was standing twenty feet away tossing its head, until the cape hung from one horn and it could see with both eyes and saw El Moro. The bull lurched at the man, who tried to plunge the sword into its neck but the sword went flying and now El Moro was embracing death and the horns tossed him upwards into the black night and eternal rest. The bull seemed to root the earth and gored and dragged the dead body, which poured its blood onto the yellow clay as the aficionados cheered, crazed with bloodlust, applauding the bull for giving them death.

Chapter Eight

The four left in silence and the girls said they were going to Mass and Hugo said they should go also. He took Carlos to the great central cathedral in the plaza, a brown monolith. It made Carlos think of something else, not a cathedral; it was more than a cathedral; it had a gigantic symbolic meaning that escaped Carlos. They went inside and he saw the Visigoth genuflect. They attended a Mass and partook of the Eucharist and listened to a choir singing liturgical music from the Spanish Middle Ages.

This is why I love Mexico, said Hugo outside. Mexico is real. Sin and death. That is what life is all about. Did you ever see anything as foreboding as our cathedral?

That was it-what Carlos was trying to say but couldn't because it didn't go with cathedrals. It was foreboding.

I agree, he said.

The matador. El matador tragico. He died a noble death this morning, said Hugo.

That's what they call them?

Yes, I'm an aficionado. An officer in our club. We have

a gallery with portraits of the matadores tragicos. There are many.

What club is that?

All aficionados, true ones, belong to clubs. We run the bullfights. My uncle will be Presidente of all the clubs in Mexico one day. He is very active. We will invite you to a function. We will have a special memorial for El Moro.

The dead matador.

Yes, soon. We will honor him.

The girls are having us over tonight and you know what that means?

No thanks. I've been through that before.

But I've agreed on your behalf. Amigo, you must do this for me. Juana would not have invited us if you weren't coming. She's only doing it because Clarita likes you. This is a very special day. You will never have another day like this.

How many men have you seen killed in the bull ring?

Five, but I go all the time. For twelve years. Only three were matadors. One was a picador and one was a clown.

You go to see people killed?

Yes, of course, but we don't think of it as that way. We think of it as La Fortuna, fate.

Death is part of it.

Yes, you understand. You are becoming a Mexican. So now you will make love to a Mexican girl.

Oh no I won't.

I bet you do.

Carlos thought of blowing it off but didn't want to destroy his friendship with Hugo. He believed Hugo could help him find Joan's killer. He enjoyed him and like learning from him. He felt Hugo had much to teach him. He planned to explain to the girl Clarita, that he was still in mourning for his wife; he was sure she would understand.

Besides, how could she possibly be in the mood for love after witnessing the horror of the man flopping like a rag doll? He remembered the blood in the sand. He was certainly in no mood for love. The death made him sick.

The girls were secretaries in an insurance agency and shared a small apartment. They served the men sangria in a colorful earthen pitcher and spoke quietly. Carlos thought they were still under the spell of the bullfight. They spoke slow enough for him to understand a little. They looked like odalisques in the candlelight- an otherworldly, paradisal reward. They wanted to know more about Carlos. They knew his wife had died and he had no children and didn't speak Spanish at home but that was about all. Then Hugo and Juana got up and left without a word and Clarita began casting her spell. She put more brandy in the Sangria and invited him to try it; it was better. Then she began telling him she liked him. He decided to get up and scram but she put slow music on and pulled him up from the couch and clung to him. They danced. Her perfume was overwhelming and her full bosom and full hard thighs pressed against him and aroused him. She felt this and began kissing him voluptuously and dug her fingers into him. He wasn't sure he knew how it happened but he ended up on the couch with her kissing him and squirming all over him, naked. He didn't want the others to catch them there and carried her to her bed. She had his clothes off in seconds and slid down between his legs. He remembered how Doris always did it the same way, but now it was different. He saw huge brown orbs and thought he was falling down a well. He was fully enveloped in flesh, full to overflowing; he seemed to ride her forever. Later, much later, she wanted to talk between kisses. I knew I would fall in love with you, tonight. I knew it all day, she said. You were so handsome at the bull ring. Such a caballero. Such a stallion. Juana is dying of jealousy. She only did it for me.

He laughed.

That's crazy. So she won't see him again.

Probably now, yes now that it's too late. Now that he has her. He's very good looking. But she won't fall in love. She knows he is a playboy. We think you are a serious boy. Did you like it?

Sure.

Do you like to do everything? We can.

I thought we did.

Oh no. This is Mexico. Why don't you rest and I'll take a shower.

He dozed and woke an hour later when he felt someone in bed and opened his eyes to see capacious buttocks rising before him.

Se preparada, she said. What the hell, he thought. When in Rome.

She squealed for joy but her voice sounded strange to him. He couldn't understand why any girl would want it. She began thrusting backwards to ask for more and he tried to get into it and then Clarita and Hugo burst in naked and laughing and Juana laughed hilariously but pleaded mas, mas, and the scene degenerated into a bacchanalian route.

Chapter Nine

The next day Hugo called him at his apartment. He assumed that Hugo would want to see the two again but he didn't. He said they were having a few drinks that night in honor of the dead matador at his club and his uncle would be there and wanted him to come.

Carlos felt bad about the girls and didn't know why. He sent them a bouquet and called them. They got on the speaker phone.

We love you, said Clarita. Both of us said Juana.

I sent you flowers.

You sweet thing.

They were speaking in Spanish and he realized he was learning it.

So will the four of us go out again?

Hugo has too many girls, said Clarita. He is a player. He says we are your new concubines. That is ok by us. Do you love us?

Sure.

Good, because we love you. We want babies.

He laughed, nervously. So they knew he had dinero.

So soon?

Yes. Please. Are you coming to see us tonight?

Sure, after I go somewhere.

With Hugo?

Yes, to a club.

Then we won't see you. He will take you away. Come tomorrow please, for dinner. We want to fix it for you. Do you like having two girls?

Sure, it's fun.

You need two because you have so much energy, so much love to give.

I want to take you out one at a time and I don't want anyone to know about us. For your sake.

So romantic, said Clarita.

I think you deserve respect. I think you're nice girls.

A caballero, said Juana.

I'll come tonight if I can get away.

They will start drinking and it will be impossible. When they start drinking they never stop. This is Mexico.

We know we were both bad last night.

Bad?

What we made you do. From behind, you know.

He smiled.

It's only for special occasions.

I can't sit down said Juana.

He thought of them as two beeves- two sleek beeves and he was el toro bravo.

Chapter Ten

Hugo was full of fun in the cab, talking about Las Concubinas. He knew a club where the two girls could get on a stage and dance naked for them. He wanted to take them. Carlos thought it was a horrible idea but didn't say anything. These girls are just for fun, said Hugo. They are like a good cigar. You can't overdo it or you don't enjoy it anymore. We will smoke very fine ones by the way. Joselito will bring them. They have been in a humidor for twenty years. His uncle had been keeping them for a special occasion, then died without smoking them. Julio y Cleopatras, the best. No, we should take these girls out perhaps every month or two. The more girls hate you, the more they love you. You said you were not a conquistador and look how you came and saw and conquered. Vini, vidi, vici. It is our motto. The motto of the conquistadores.

Will someone marry these girls?

Oh, yes, many would but they don't want poor Mexicans or old fat men with bald heads. They want to have fun. As much as they can. Then they will have babies and get fat.

They asked me for babies.

When Hugo heard this he laughed all the way to the next intersection where he turned into the parking lot of the Circulo de Madrid. The club was a sprawling affair with a Spanish garden and a fountain in a central courtyard, a meeting room, dining room and a ballroom for parties. Carlos looked for signs that the Club was recognizing the death and saw black crepe around a large photo of the dead matador as they entered. They found Senor Gutierez in the courtyard smoking a cigar, sitting by himself and meditating. He made Carlos think of a senator. He smiled and stood up to shake hands.

The famous cigars, he said. I have two for you. We must smoke them in honor of Joselito's uncle and El Moro. He died a noble death. You knew he had cancer?

I heard the rumor, said Hugo. Do you think that's why he asked for the bull?

Of course.

Will they let it fight again? asked Carlos.

Oh, yes. It's already been selected by Cordovas. He will fight it in a month.

Has a bull ever killed two matadors? asked Carlos.

Oh yes, in Barcelona in 1972. One bull killed three. And many more bulls have survived to fight again. This bull is local. Gigante. The pride of Mexico. Cordovas is one of the top five matadors in the world. He will come here from Spain.

Do they train these bulls to kill men? asked Carlos.

Oh, yes. With dummies. The best bulls have earned millions for their owners. And the betting is astronomical now. Hundreds of millions will be bet on this bull. This was only his second fight. He is a young bull and people are betting on him to survive or to kill. Everyone I know will bet on him. I do not think he will kill Cordovas but they will have a hard time killing him.

Carlos realized that he was in the Middle Ages and Latin men were completely insane. He saw how it could get into your blood.

So yes Carlos, I have something to report, said Gutierez.

I am making inquiries about the numbered accounts. I don't know what's in them but my people tell me that no one else seems to have access to them.

Carlos wondered who his people were. He realized that Gutierez was well worth his ten percent.

This bodes well for us. I think it will go as easy as I had hoped.

Do you think I'm safe here, asked Carlos.

As safe as I can make you. After a time I will change your identity and move you somewhere else- a small silver town near here. To Taxco. I like to visit it.

But what about the important matter? said Carlos. Joan.

It is only important to you. It is not important to me and I want you to accept that we may not be able to do anything about it.

Carlos looked incredulous.

This is not a fantasy world of justice for all. Be patient. I think we may stumble onto something. My people are making inquiries.

The sums involved are so great, said Carlos.

No, they are paltry. Everything is billions today. These sums are piddling in the world of crime.

So you are convinced she was involved in crime, asked Carlos.

Why else would she be dead? commented Gutierez.

They went into a ballroom where a hundred mature men had gathered to commemorate El Moro. Speeches were given; Hugo gave one. Carlos noted that he was understanding more Spanish. The speeches were slow and dignified. He found if he knew the subject it was getting easy for him to understand the Spanish. He kept hearing the same words-valor, genius, our brother, a hero, a brave bull. The men were mostly over 60 and solemn. They drank scotch or sherry from Spain. Carlos and Hugo drank sparingly but the old men were runaway trains and in a couple hours they were baracho. Hugo introduced Carlos to all of them. Everyone thought he was Latin and were too drunk to discern his Spanish was not a Mexican's.

Then Hugo asked him to leave with him.

I have something to show you, he said. A delicacy. Carlos wondered if it was something to eat. He was getting hungry. Hugo drove twenty five minutes into the Pink Zone to a café. Here she is, he said, as they approached the hat check. Carlos thought the hat check girl was the most adorable Latin girl he had ever seen, petite, pure white skin, lovely twinkling brown eyes, blue-black hair, a smile that made him weak. She recognized Hugo and presented her cheek to be kissed. He introduced Carlos who kissed her hand; she was gracious and charming-poised from dealing with the public. The hostess took them to a table. Rich smells of food and flowers; classical guitar music. She will marry in a couple weeks, said Hugo.

I can understand that.

She is poor of course and will marry a minor government official-someone in the Minister of Interior. It will be a good marriage for her.

Good, said Carlos. She's a nice girl.

Yes, she likes you.

Carlos laughed.

Why shouldn't she? You're handsome and rich. This is obvious. So she will marry in a couple weeks and then she will be mine.

Carlos thought of his own wife and was not amused.

Don't worry. You'll be next in line.

How could you get tired of a girl like this?

Yes, isn't it amazing? I find it amazing myself. Uncle tells me that I mustn't get involved in your affairs but I must tell you I'm dying of curiosity- I mean about your wife.

It killed the cat, said Carlos. You are already trying to find a husband to kill you.

A riposte; good. I'm sharpening your intellect. Did you figure out what evidence you already had? Hidden in your past?

No, I can't come up with anything.

Well, you must let me help you.

I agree. I don't think your uncle's heart is in it. Alright, let me think. So basically this is what happened: my wife died in a suspicious hit and run. Then McMahon, my lawyer in Grand Cayman was killed the same way: so I had to believe it was murder. So I found a baggage claim and Royal Leeds with a twelve digit number in this fancy reptile purse. I though she must have been to Cayman and got the purse there because I had never seen a purse like it anywhere. It must have cost a fortune. So I found out she had millions in banks in Cayman and all over. She would be gone for three even four day weekends with her mother. Except her mother told me she was really with men. She was like a high-priced call girl.

A cortesana.

Yes, but I can't believe that's how she got the money and it wouldn't explain why she was murdered.

I agree. So what kind of men?

Her mother said older, wealthy men. I got the impression they were local.

So what was she doing? said Hugo.

I assumed they were taking her on trips.

53

Perhaps she was doing something associated with the millions.

But what?

Well, we've got one interesting theory to work with already.

We do?

Yes, she was trading in wild animal parts.

Carlos looked at him, open-mouthed.

The purse, he said.

The traffic in wild animal hides alone accounts for billions. Get me some good photos of the purse and I'll tell you.

So, what would she be doing? asked Carlos.

Moving money around most likely. Maybe she was keeping some money in the process. She may have been. Or maybe we're all wet and it was something else. Get me the photos. They have to be good ones. Tampa is becoming a hub for trade with Latin America. Like Miami.

But where do we go from there?

I don't know. At least it's a first step. On second thought, forget the photos: send the purse. Photos are an approximation of color and color is a very subtle matter. Also, the color may not be enough. We may need the hide.

They ate charusco steaks and Hugo talked bulls and said the odds against the bull killing Cordova were three to eight and he thought they would drop to one to four and when they did he was putting a grand on the bull. Carlos couldn't believe his ears.

So how would you feel if you won four grand?

Great. It's not like you think. I will not be cheering for the bull. I would spend it on a needy person, probably Rosa. I think I'm in love with her.

Carlos laughed. Now I know why you're not married.

I'm in too much demand here. As are you. There is absolutely no money here. So for a girl like Rosa it could mean the difference between living in a small apartment and having a real home.

But what would she tell her husband?

She won the lottery.

Carlos was mortified-it made him think of the jewels.

So the matador's death is in the scheme of things, said Hugo. He wants to face this death. What did Mozart say? The greatest composer. He loved death and longed for it? The bull fighter has a mystical relationship with death. This has nothing to do with my bet. But I will not mourn him or feel bad. I will feel good because he was blessed with a noble death from a great bull. If our bull kills Cordova he will be a great bull. I feel he will do it. The way he killed El Moro. You did not understand what you saw. After you have watched a thousand bullfights you will understand.

This is very hard for an American to deal with, said Carlos. Especially the betting.

Yes, but you are no longer one. You are a Mexican and a conquistador. So what do you want to do. See the girls? Are you willing to share your concubines with a friend? Don't get them pregnant. They would become big as whales. They will appreciate us more if we stay away a few weeks. Then they will be like lambs. Besides I am in love with Rosa. I say we go to the bar at the Cinco de Mayo.

On their way out the hat check girl pressed a note into Hugo's hand. They got into Hugo's Mercedes and sped away. You don't want to know what it says? Hugo asked.

It's not my business.

You have very fine manners. The manners of a Conquistador. She wants to see me.

What does she want?

Money, of course.

But I thought…

Yes, but she probably has something else in mind. Another way to show her love. The problem is one gets carried away. She's getting off in a couple hours. That gives us a chance to check out the Cinco de Mayo.

It was a busy lounge and tapas restaurant. Intoxicating smells. Ambiance of Spain. The girls there reminded Carlos of the two that were waiting for him.

Hugo talked bulls then began talking about his love for Rosa. He hated to let her get married when he loved her so much and she wanted to be his girlfriend but he knew himself too well. He had to assume he would tire of her; then what would he do with her?

She's not in love with her future husband? asked Carlos.

I don't know. You never know. You can't believe anything they say. Sometimes they don't know themselves. All I know is that the waiting is driving me crazy. I really love the girl.

Well, don't go then. You might do something you wish you hadn't.

Yes, there's an excellent chance of that actually. But she'll cry her eyes out if I don't come. Maybe I should take you along, give her some pesos and leave. If you're there I won't be able to do anything.

Right, like last night. You are really a funny guy, Hugo.

I never try to be funny. No, this is different. I'm in love with Rosa. So lets go over and pick her up at her job. She'll be off in fifteen to twenty minutes.

She came out and jumped into the Mercedes sports car and sat in Carlos's lap. Her perfume and effervescence made his head spin. She wanted to go to Hugo's condo but he begged off saying that he had to take Carlos somewhere. She wanted Carlos to meet her sister. She made Carlos give her his cell number and said she'd have Lola call him. Carlos decided to get a new phone but would have to clear it with Gutierez. They left her and Hugo said they might as well stop off at Juana and Clarita's.

Someone had to put them to bed. It was past twelve, but the girls were delighted to see the two conquistadors and the melee of the previous night was reenacted.

Chapter Eleven

Two days later the lizard purse arrived from Tampa and the two men drove it to the University of Mexico. Carlos recognized the famous Aztec Mosaic. They took it to the biology department and found a reptile expert in a cluttered office full of papers and specimens. He studied the purse intently, looked at it under a magnifying glass, scraped it and examined it under a microscope for dye and found none. He appeared stumped. He said he would talk to some colleagues and get back to them. Hugo tried to talk to him about a fee but he said he wasn't interested in one. A couple days later he called Hugo and said it was a protected species of lizard that had last been seen in the Central Amazon. It was not known whether it was extinct. He said the extraordinary beauty of the blue-gray hide would allow it to command an enormous price. He knew a little about the trade in illegal wild animal skins and knew that the hides came primarily from South America and Africa. Where was it manufactured? Near the source, was the professor's guess. Very little was known about it but he thought that no one with any sense would ship the hides somewhere to be cured and assembled when the shipment could be interdicted. Why not have the artisans work near the source?

Hugo called Carlos. They met at Rosa's tapas bar so Hugo could kill two birds with one stone-talk to Carlos and Rosa. Carlos had a map of Brazil.

I have seen purses like this in the city but nothing this fine, he said.

Women are insane for purses, as you know. So what would some oil sheik's wife pay for this? I shudder to think. I want to give it to Rosa by the way.

Sure.

Alright. It was hunted in the Central Amazon, but there's not much in the way of civilization near its habitat. He drew a circle. So where did they take this hide to make the purse? Amazonia, the capital, is inland, but my instincts tell me they took it to Rio.

The biggest city?

Right. Millions of inhabitants. A helluva place to look for a shop.

I don't know, said Carlos. Say you went there and had mucho dinero and asked to see a selection of rare purses. Maybe you could pay off the vendor to take you to the workshop.

I think it's a good way to get yourself killed.

Alright. I go to Rio and I find out where it was made. How does that help me find the man who killed my wife?

I don't know. One step at a time. What do you know about these men?

Nothing, said Carlos.

You must have some thoughts.

I can't prove anything, said Carlos.

You don't start by proving anything, said Hugo. You start with a theory.

I think it all began with a pawnbroker named Mizrahi.

He gave her jewelry. She wanted a will and went to these lawyers. The senior partner talked about her wonderful inner quality. I think he fucked her and turned his wealthy clients onto her.

And that's how she met the dealer?

Of course. It has to be that way. So someone is managing this business in Brazil. That person will lead us back to the party in Tampa and he will be the murderer.

Except it won't be that easy, said Hugo. Not necessarily. The question will be whether he communicates directly with Brazil. If I were a big investor in Tampa I would do all I could to insulate myself from this operation. I wouldn't repatriate any of the money I earned from it. I would keep it off shore.

So I need to go to Rio and look for a source of rare purses.

You? I didn't know you spoke Portuguese.

I don't. I'd have to learn, I guess. You're not telling me you want to get yourself killed over my wife?

I can't let you go on your own. You're not ready.

But you're not going to spout this Superman talk in Brazil?

Only with fellow Visigoths like you, but then you must take it with a grain of salt. You know I love everyone. Speaking of which, that's Rosa's sister Lola talking to her. They could almost be twins. I've got to get out of town before I give in to Rosa. She's begging me and I'm losing my resolve. Now they see me looking at them and they're coming over . Lola must be a virgin too. Of course. They're good Catholic girls. Actually I love both of them.

The girls wanted to go dancing and they went to a club that featured reggae and emphasized slow dances and Lola clung to him. He became aroused and was sure she could feel his arousal and was responding by pressing against him. She sat close to him between dances and kept holding his hand and gazing lovingly into his eyes, smiling. She had just graduated from high school and was working in a department store and living with her parents. Both sisters were.

It's such a tragedy, she said. How they are in love, but can't marry.

Why not?

In Mexico we have social classes. Not like the United States. We are so behind. Hugo is from one of the families. They only marry each other and own everything.

Including girls?

If a girl is lucky enough. That is why she worked at her job. Hoping she would meet her dream.

He is making her marry but she doesn't want it. Her husband is awful. He's overweight.

So a girl takes whatever she can get?

She must. There's so little opportunity. Mexico is so poor . So you don't have a girl.

He thought of how he had two.

No.

I would date you. I know you like me.

Yes, I do.

I'm 18.

Rosa said you were twenty. I didn't believe it.

I never smoke cigarettes and I don't drink much.

I notice.

Why don't we date?

Alright, said Carlos. When I get back.

Where are you going?

I can't tell you.

When are you leaving?

Soon.

Then we can date until you leave.

That might not be a good idea. I might not come back.

Then I want to come too.

I mean I might be killed.

She looked devastated.

Then you mustn't go

I have to. Now I've been an idiot and run my mouth. I can't drink anymore.

I have to know. It's so mysterious. Please tell me.

It's too dangerous. It's funny. I try not to think about girls. You wouldn't be interested in me. I get involved with girls and can't get rid of them. It happened last night.

I know, she laughed. Las Concubinas. I don't care about them. They can't compete with me and Rosa.

He noticed the "and Rosa". So they knew Hugo would wander off in time and leave them with him. If he didn't get out of town he'd end up with more of Hugo's girls. He thought of himself and the concubines in an amorous heap-a more or less nightly occurrence. Enough was enough.

Hugo saw her interest in Carlos as serendipitous. He felt sure that this would make Lola and Rosa as accessible to him as Clarita and Juana. He wanted to do everything to encourage consummation. He genuinely liked Carlos and thought that Lola would help him get over the loss of his wife. As for Rio, he saw their chances of them finding the source of the purses there as negligible- he wanted to go to the Carnival in Rio because he hadn't been to one in several years. The big thing was to make Carlos think he was doing all he could until he got back to normal and got over his bereavement.

Unlike Rosa, Lola had no prospect of marriage on the

horizon. Surely, if Lola got to him, he would fall in love with her. Consequently, when she asked Hugo where Carlos lived, he did not stop at giving her Carlos's address; he drove her there in his car. It was a couple days later. Carlos had not returned her phone messages and was planning to leave for Rio in a week. He thought that Hugo was waiting for a scheduled hearing; in fact he was waiting for Carnival. No one knew where he lived and Carlos assumed it was someone from the building when he opened the door. She squealed with joy and threw her arms around him. He didn't know what to do and returned her embrace. Then she was pulling him by the hand from room to room of his expensively appointed apartment and effervescing. She opened the fridge and wanted to look into all the kitchen cabinets and found a wine cellar. She selected a Spanish red and wine glasses and they sat in the living room on the couch drinking.

Why is your apartment more luxurious than Hugo's? You must be richer.

I don't know anything about him.

He's very rich. Or his family is.

He looked at her thoughtfully. She was really very different than her sister. She was more coquettish; a wiggle worm. She knew how desirable he found her and turned on her airs and graces, her most seductive ones- she kept showing him her pretty pink tongue as she talked, she found endless ways to display it and torment and entice him with it. She was wearing a pinkish blouse that made him think of lingerie, and he became gradually aware that she was braless and her bosom was moving freely beneath it.

I'm not going to let you leave me to go to Rio until you tell me everything.

How can I trust you?

Because I like you. I want to date you, remember? Don't

you know what that means, when a Mexican girl wants that?

No.

It means she is very serious.

But I told you I had the two.

She smiled slyly. But if I say they don't matter, she began.

How could they not matter?

They're a joke; they're much too old for you. They can't interest you long. I don't care about them. I just want to live with you here.

He laughed nervously. She was just too beautiful. Would she actually surrender her most precious asset to shack with a young millionaire who might fall in love with her and marry her. He thought he was reasonably sure of the answer. The problem was that he wanted her. She was vastly more desirable to him than the others.

So why does my boyfriend have to go to Rio? she asked. He broke down and told her the whole story and she began laughing.

Don't you know what happens in a couple weeks in Rio?

No, said Carlos.

It's famous all over Latin America. Rio is famous for it. Carnival. Hugo just wants to go to Carnival. Looking for one shop in Rio? That would be like looking for a single grain of sand on the sea shore. And why Rio? There are many cities all over Brazil big enough to have a shop like this. Hugo is a fox.

I'm so stupid. I haven't looked on a map. Let's do it.

They went to his bedroom and called it up on a computer and he felt like an idiot. She sat on his lap and looked with him.

But I would still go there. I think it would be the most likely place.

I'll let you go for a week, she said.

Then you're coming back to me. And I'm staying here, starting tonight.

But, you're a virgin.

Don't you think I should have the right to give my virginity away when I want?

She began kissing him and he was swept out to sea.

He realized that he had just met her and knew nothing about her. He remembered how he had spent six months getting to know everything about his wife. She was brighter than he was- he knew that much. He had felt the same way about Joan.

Don't you believe in love at first sight, she said.

Yes, I fell in love that way.

With your wife?

He didn't answer.

I will be your next wife. She must have been a beautiful Spanish girl. But not as beautiful as me. No girl's as beautiful as me. I know you're in love, know how?

Tell me.

Because of how I could feel you when we were dancing.

This of course had recurred.

And I feel it again. So you can't say no.

I can't?

No. I won't let you. So don't get any ideas because I already know everything.

But what if we can't get along.

We have to get along.

Oh, why's that?

Because you are the man here and I have to always obey-which I want to anyway. So you see. We can't fight. Don't your concubines always obey?

He had never thought about it but they were virtually servants.

Of course they do, because this is Mexico. I know you want to see my breasts.

I do? Yes. You noticed I have no bra on. You kept noticing. Why don't you undress me and take me to bed? She stood up and pulled him to bed. They sat on the bed a moment side by side and he was at a loss. He didn't want to do it but he was ready to explode;

She smiled excitedly and took his hands and put them on her blouse and he unbuttoned the top button. She kissed his hands and looked at him, worshipfully.

I know you're in love with me. Please say you are. See. I told you.

She took his hands and held them to her chest and he found himself unbuttoning the rest of her buttons and opening her blouse and staring entranced at her perfection.

You can kiss them, she said. He got a little excited and seconds later they were out of their clothes and tearing at one another. He expected to feel the subtle resistance he felt on his marriage night but didn't. An amorous free-for all ensued. She got up at one point and went to the bathroom and he noticed the sheet- it was as white as a sheet. He wondered if Hugo had gotten there before he had. He felt a sense of relief. The girl had gone on about it, said how wonderful it was being deflowered. Now they could get married as soon as he got back from Rio. He could be gone a week. No longer. He compared the experience to lovemaking with the concubines. He lost himself in them and was enveloped. This was more exciting- a sort of erotic contest between equals. His level of excitement and arousal was far greater. Excitement. That was the thing. She was much more exciting-constantly changing, delighting, surprising. He knew he would fall in love with her. He fell asleep in her arms and had a dream that he was on a moonless sea sailing noiselessly toward a distant shore. Then he heard festive music, with horns and drums growing louder and saw a riot of colors and colored faces, samba music; he was at Carnival in Rio and he was dancing with a woman with orange-brown skin and a headdress of resplendent feathers. I knew you would come for me, she said. He woke and realized that it was Joan, that she had come back and was waiting for him. He believed he would find her in Rio. He left for Rio the next morning. Lola woke to find herself in an empty bed

Chapter Twelve

Carlos arrived in the city at ten o'clock that night and stayed at an ultra modern hotel on Copacabana beach. He woke early in the morning, ate, went for a swim with the beach empty; bright, crystalline day, took a cab around the city. He asked the driver where he could get the most expensive women's clothes in town. He wanted to buy a gift. He hoped to find the purses and trace them to the supplier. The driver took him to an exclusive strip of fashionable boutiques. He got out and began browsing in a store. This made him feel awkward; being the only man in the store other than the clerks. He dressed expensively and got a lot of attention from the clerks, especially the girls. A couple flirted with him; one asked him out and gave him her card. He saw nothing anywhere that looked anything like wild animal parts and decided to give up on the boutique. He spent two days buying expensive items in stores and asking to see the most expensive purses available in the city for his mother's birthday. He assumed that if anyone had what he was looking for they wouldn't display it openly. On the third day he was lunching in a café when he saw two chic women sitting several tables away. The woman nearest him had a wide belt made from an animal that made him think of an ocelot-yellow, with black spots. She wore a dress and had a purse that he recognized as a three thousand dollars Hermes purse from one of the boutiques. When the two got up he followed them at a distance. They went into a skyscraper a block away and took an elevator. He looked at the directory in the lobby and saw the logo of a boutique named Giorgios on the ninth floor. He took the elevator and went inside the store. They were not there. He bought some handkerchiefs and toiletries and left an hour later. He asked about expensive purses for his mother and was directed to the twelfth floor. They were coming out of an unmarked office with packages as he got off the elevator. He noted the number on the door. They got into the elevator. He waited for the next and saw them on the sidewalk turning a corner and made chase. He caught them just as they were going into a boutique and took up a post across the street on the terrace of a café and waited an hour for them to come out. When they came out they had more packages. They came over to the café and sat at his table. The blonde with the belt was now wearing a forest green leather jacket. She smiled warmly and asked him in Portuguese why he had been following them. He didn't understand her, guessed, but guessed right, and responded in Spanish that gentlemen preferred blondes. She laughed. It was the only thing he could think of.

You seem like a nice boy, she said in Spanish. I wish I could believe you.

I'm telling the truth. You can polygraph me.

She laughed again.

Well I'm so flattered.

I'm sure it happens all the time, he said.

I think he's telling the truth, said her brunette friend. An agency wouldn't hire an American.

How did you know I'm American? Of course, it's my Spanish.

Your American accent. So you like blondes. Well I'm flattered. Where are you from?

Miami.

You've come for Carnival?

Yes.

I love the way you dress. So European for an American. But you're only a teenager. Are you here with your parents.

Actually, I'm twenty one.

And you like blondes. That's nice. Where are you staying?

On Copacabana Beach.

So you like to watch the girls?

I just got here yesterday. I went swimming before anyone was at the beach.

So I'm … Susan and this is Lora.

Well, I suppose you will want to call me now that you've hunted me down. We noticed you at the restaurant when we came out together. It was a little scary. But Lora said he's just a teenager let's see what he wants. You were dressed so nicely. So give me your room and I'll come for you tonight at nine o'clock. You don't know Rio. This will be fun showing you around. I am really flattered, really I am. So, where is your girlfriend?

I don't have one.

It was obvious to him that she liked that. They presented their hands to be kissed and said ciao bambino and carried their burdens to a waiting cab where they threw kisses to him through the window. Why was she coming to pick him up? She was probably married. He thought of her as hot; she reminded him of Bianca Jagger. Maybe she would tell him where she bought the belt so he could buy one for his mother. He planned to tell her that his money came from his mother's divorce. His parents were Cuban but they didn't speak Spanish. His grandparents had come from Havana and his father was a successful business man.

She showed up at the appointed hour dressed in a skin tight black dress that showed her striking figure. She seemed surprised that he was actually there, in an expensive room, alone.

Why don't you shave? she asked. It's the fashion now.

Actually, I think I like it.

He decided to grow a beard so he could always disappear by shaving. He looked different, like someone else, with the black stubble. He had also cut his hair and it was black again.

She smelt like something very expensive and rare. It had to be some of the dearest perfume money could buy. So wouldn't she be the sort that bought the purses? He thought of asking her about the belt but had the sense not to; it might arouse suspicion. She had a cab waiting that took them to an intimate piano bar about twenty minutes from his hotel. They drank martinis and listened to Latin jazz, pianissimo and understated. She had a hundred questions but said nothing about her own life. Married, thought Carlos.

You don't smoke, she said suddenly. I'm trying to give it up but I'm dying for one.

Please do, he said.

She allowed him to light her cigarette and took a deep drag, exhaled and looked at him alluringly.

So now that you've got your blonde, what are you going to do with her?

He couldn't think for a moment.

Do you want to date? he stammered.

I think that's what we're doing, dear. I find you irresistible. I still can't believe you ran me down.

I didn't think I was stalking you.

I'm not complaining.

Then she heard something she wanted to dance to and they began dancing slowly. It occurred to him that he should ask her to come with him to pick out clothes. This might get her talking about clothes and she might tell him where she got the belt. She danced in a lady-like way but pressed closer during the second dance.

I feel so comfortable with you, dear, but I don't think we should go back to your hotel. I know a little place not far from here.

I couldn't ask you to do anything on our first date, he said.

Such a gentleman, she responded. But maybe I want to.

This meant to him that she had a jealous husband. She had him in the backseat of a cab speeding to a hotel, nestling against him, squeezing his hand in hers. He imagined a husband killing him before he could accomplish anything. She took him to a small hotel where people rented rooms by the hour to have sex with prostitutes. She began kissing him as soon as they got into the room. I'm so afraid of falling in love, she said. I know what you want and of course I want you to have it, but the way you danced with me I just went crazy. I could feel you. You're such a hot boy, a big boy. She felt him intimately. They were naked in seconds and she looked like she lived at a spa but he was put off by her breast implants, which were overdone. She fell to her knees from their embrace and began fellating him. He thought he was making a porno flick. She seemed totally devoid of femininity, tawdry and false. It was worse than Doris. Then she was in bed on her back, legs back, pulling him down into her, responding vigorously while narrating. She said she was either having an orgasm or building to one; she kept him fully advised. An hour later she had had two and someone began pounding on the door. Suddenly she and her husband were screaming at each other in Portuguese. Carlos hastily dressed and opened the window. There was some kind of half-assed metal ladder that ended a story off the ground. He began descending these steps which were almost rusted through and one gave way under his feet and then another. He could hear the husband in the room. The fool began firing shots out the window; Carlos could see the hand and the orange blasts from the pistol but fortunately the shooter did not look down to see Carlos hanging there. Bastardo! Cobardo! The screaming went on for awhile then subsided and Carlos pulled himself up into the window and saw the couple coupling and ducked down again. He had a foothold and a handhold and managed to cling to it until they left. He got a cab and went back to his hotel where he changed rooms fearing the woman would return.

Chapter Thirteen

The next day he relaxed on the beach and watched the topless beauties, swam, and thought about his next move. It occurred to him that the woman might come looking for him and he would be wise to get a new hotel. He moved a few hotels down the beach to an even newer and more deluxe hotel. So Hugo was right; he wasn't ready. He had almost gotten himself killed. In just a few days. But it had not been for naught. He remembered the door the two had emerged from with packages.

The next day he sat on the terrace across the street from the building trying to read a paper in Portuguese. It looked like Spanish but didn't sound like Spanish . He had decided to be more cautious, to make sure he knew what was going on before he made a move. He would sit there until a truck and delivery man with the right profile went inside, follow him and then go shopping in the building. The following day he saw clothing on a rack go in but thought it must be for the boutique, Giorgios, and sat tight. On the third day a brunette sat down beside him smiling warmly.

I was sure I'd find you here.

Lora?

So you had quite an adventure. Sue has been looking for you. She was quite impressed.

I hope things are ok with her and her husband.

Oh, yes. It's breathed new life into their relationship. He's beating her again.

He laughed nervously.

That's a good thing. It means he hasn't lost interest in her. He had stopped. He doesn't actually injure her. So you must be looking for another blonde. Can't find any on the beach?

He tried to smile.

Sue actually thought you were telling the truth.

I was.

Please, dear. If I dyed my hair blonde, would you stalk me?

You wouldn't have to.

Well, I like that. So you like mature women?

You're not much older than me.

So gallant. And mysterious. Whatever are you looking for, dear?

Looking for?

Don't tell me. I don't care. I'm not afraid so you can stalk me all you want. And my husband's not jealous. I could take you home. You can't be serious?

Yes. What are you doing tonight?

I'm free actually.

Oh, Sue will die. She says she's in love. Well I want to fall in love too.

I don't want you to tell her. And I'd rather pick you up.

Of course. You won't get to meet my lord and master. I'm afraid he's out of the country.

She hastily wrote down her address. She reminded him of the old posters of an Italian movie star. Was it the more famous one or the other one? He thought it was the other one, Gina something. She presented her cheek to be kissed and left to get in a cab, swinging her full hips freely-she was much better looking than her friend, more natural looking. He liked her big eyes and mouth with pouty lips and marveled at her amplitude. He put her in her early forties.

She would show him her bedroom and he might get a chance to see her clothes. He dressed in a black Armani suit and showed up at her door at the appointed hour-nine that night. She had a sprawling one story in a gated community with a small station for security in the front yard. A man with a shotgun came out, looked at him and went back in. Carlos thought of it as a wooden shack. He saw these stations up and down the street and wondered if they all had men with shotguns in them. She answered the door, looked and smelt beautiful. She said that she had fixed something special and wanted a quiet evening alone. He heard classical guitar playing. Remembrances of Alhambra. She showed him the living room which was immense, then took him to an intimate den with lavish red velvet that set off her raven hair, pure white skin and carmine lips. She had champagne in a bucket and hors d'oeuvres on a silver charger. She asked him to pop the cork. He filled two flutes.

To amor, she said toasting; their glasses rang. He liked the champagne. Love must be something you know about, she said.

Not really.

Then you need a teacher. I'm sorry about Sue and what happened. You must have been afraid for your life.

I was pretty scared. I was holding onto this fire escape that was falling apart on me.

You poor dear. They play games. I don't do that. It's so stupid what they do.

So you don't want to be beaten.

Oh, no, are you one of those?

I would never beat a woman.

Good. But I'm still afraid of you.

Afraid?

Yes, of what you can do to my heart. I'm afraid that if I become your lover I will fall in love. You'll leave me of course.

We can be friends, I mean, forever.

Is that what you want?

Oh no, I'm very attracted to you.

He knew what she wanted him to say.

And I don't get tired of girls.

Girls. I like being a girl. And you never hit one?

No, I wouldn't.

So I want to know all about you. What are your interests?

He didn't have any and wondered if he should make one up.

I'm just an average guy. I like sports.

You play them?

No. Just watch.

American sports. Football?

And basketball. I was going to college. I wanted to learn business.

Good. And girls. You must have had an interest in girls.

Sure. But nothing serious. I had a couple girlfriends.

Sue was very impressed. I'm not going to tell her about us. I don't think she'd appreciate it. She said you're a good dancer. She picked up her remote and changed the music to a slow piece of American jazz and came over to him and took his hand.

Show me, she said pulling him up. She clung to him and put her head on his shoulder.

After a couple dances she looked up at him smiling and opened her lips to be kissed. He kissed her and she didn't want to stop. She wanted him to take over, but he was too shy so she sat beside him on the couch and fed him hors d'oeuvres with dainty white fingers.

I'm yours, dear, she said. I'm putty in your hands. He understood that she was saying she wanted to make love. That's why he had come. His object was her boudoir.

Should I carry you to bed? he asked.

Oh, no. I don't want to wear you out.

She led him to her bedroom which made him think of a movie-set more red velvet, a huge Mediterranean style bed. She had him sit on it and sat on his lap and kissed slowly. She wanted him to appreciate her wonders, which were generous. He was stunned momentarily, watching them unfold as he undressed. She sat beside him and helped him, then gazed lovingly into his eyes. He remembered Hugo and realized he was there to conquer her and make her his slave and abettor. He decided to give her everything he had, the works. He thought he knew what women wanted from his experience with the concubinas and grazed on her like an animal feeding-a starving one. It was all hokum but she believed it. She stopped him when he got to her essence, covering herself with two modest little hands. He pulled them away and continued voraciously and didn't mount her until she was convulsing in orgasm.

I knew it would be like this, she said as he began pounding her. Oh, yes, yes, What are you going to do with me? Oh, it's so good.

I'm trying to make you my girl, he said.

Yes, tuyas. It is yours.

He kept her up late into the night, made her do everything; she fell asleep in his amorous embrace.

Sue would die, she said at breakfast the next morning. They sat at a table in a huge country kitchen. He noticed he hadn't seen the first servant.

She was so wrong to take you there and let her husband find you.

Maybe she didn't know, he said.

Of course she did. He always tails her. There are always ways, but she took a chance. I think she wanted to get caught to get back at him. Now, she's sorry. If she knew about us; she'd die.

Well, don't tell her.

Oh, I won't, believe me. Well, you certainly made full use of me last night. I can still feel it. So now that I'm yours what will you do with me?

Enjoy as much of you as I can.

As much as you did last night?

Yes; It was wonderful.

I'm glad you agree.

But we can't do it every night. I mean with your situation. Being married.

I can't remember a night like that. Are you an athlete?

I was in high school. I ran the last lap of the relay.

Yes a dash, she said dreamily.

I've got a function tonight, but I can't bear the thought of leaving you.

I can't bear it either. I want to go to a new movie. You wouldn't like it. You can come by my hotel later if you want. I want to take a bath. Why don't we take one together?

He wanted to see her clothes.

He carried her to her bedroom and removed her lingerie.

I want to see more of it, he said. I love too see you wear it. I want you to wear more for me.

He followed her into her vast-size closet and she looked into a chest and took out a black panties and bras and put them on. He said it turned him on and she could see his arousal and was delighted and wanted to act but he wouldn't let her. He stopped her and made her put on something else and said he would look for things he wanted her to wear for him and found a leather jacket which had a fur collar that reminded him of the belt. Where did you get this cool coat? I've never seen anything like it. I want you to wear it.

Like this, naked?

Yes.

He put it on her, turned her around, then took it off and put it back on the hanger. He would ask her to take him to the store. Then he had her try on a pink slip and carried her to the Jacuzzi and stripped her and put her in the water and sat on the deck and let her go crazy. She kept trying to take more.

You have to relax, he said. Don't try so hard. You're the very best when you don' try.

I get so excited, she said. I want to give you everything. When you started talking about taking a bath I got wet.

I'm going to keep you wet. He let her bathe him then carried her to the bed and mounted her and rode her until she cried uncle.

Then she got a call from Sue. He was sure she would have to tell her girlfriend what she was up to; he imagined them together gossiping. He said he needed to get back to his hotel. She dropped him off and sped away to join her girlfriend.

Chapter Fourteen

Carlos returned to his post on the terrace and watched for delivery men. After a couple hours he saw an unmarked truck stop and saw a man take in a large box in brown paper. He left money on the table and walked across the street in time to get on the elevator with him. Ninth floor. The man left the elevator and a moment later Carlos saw the man knock at the door. Carlos ducked back in the elevator, descended and tried to hail a cab, but they were all occupied. A minute later the delivery man was getting into his truck. Traffic was heavy; Carlos wondered if he could keep up with the truck on foot. He walked briskly for a block then jogged, then it got on a six lane road and he found himself sprinting. It would have gotten away had it not been for a red light. He noticed a cab at a curb, jumped in and told the cab driver he was sightseeing. He was afraid to tell him to follow the truck. When it turned into a warehouse district he asked the cab driver to follow a few blocks then got out when he saw it pull into a warehouse. Carlos walked past the warehouse and realized he couldn't be seen loitering there. He studied the neighborhood and wondered where he could take up his post. He went back to his hotel and tried to formulate a plan. Girls would be working in the factory and would get off work around five. He could try to hook up with one of the girls and get in that way. Maybe she could get him a job. He needed to dress way down. He moved out of his hotel and into a transient hotel and found cheap clothes in a thrift store. The next day he had a cab drive by the warehouse at five o'clock.

No one came out. He took another one about a half hour later and saw three girls leave work and walk to a bus stop. He got out of the cab and chased the bus a couple stops and got on but did not look at the girls. Of course they saw him get on and sit down. He got off with one of them when she got off the bus twenty minutes later. Now they were in a slum, tin roofs and cement block houses.

He followed her at a distance and saw her go into one. An hour later she left with a large plastic container and went to get water from an outlet a couple blocks away. He asked to carry it back for her and she smiled and let him. She made Doris look like Marilyn Monroe. He asked if she was doing anything that night. She took him home and introduced him to her family-ten people including grandparents and small children. She said come back at nine o'clock and they could go for a walk and have a drink. Her name was Marisol. Marisol said she was twenty one and had a child that was four- a little boy who went on the walk with them to a bar. She was on the heavy side. He told her he needed a job; did she know anyone who could give him one? He would sweep the floors; he didn't care. She said there were no jobs right then. He asked her about her job and she said it didn't pay well. They made clothes out of leather and fur-all ladies clothes, jackets, belts, purses, shoes, anything made out of leather- and blankets from fur, Sometimes they made blankets. Could she get him a job there? He was from

Mexico. She said she would ask. He said he couldn't "speak good" because he was a little retarded.

She left the child for an hour with a girlfriend and said she knew a place where they could make love. If no one was around. He said it was unnecessary. He liked her as a person and it was their first date. She said no, no, it was alright, he was a cool dude and she knew how guys were; how they always wanted to do it.

She took him to a dump and saw that the night watchman hadn't come to work and took him to an abandoned car, a little rotted out Japanese car without wheels, and opened the back door. It had a ratty back seat. She said they could do it on the back seat. Didn't he want to kiss her first? She pulled him inside and started kissing and she took him out and fellated him and then hiked up her dress and offered herself. She put a condom on him with pudgy fingers and he mounted her from behind so he didn't have to see her face. Afterwards she said she liked it and definitely wanted to be with him. They couldn't come there every night but she knew another place they might be able to go. The problem was people. There were always people around. He came back to see her every night for three days and said to keep asking at work. He would sweep and clean for half the regular pay. He was from Mexico and would be happy to get anything. A week later she said her supervisor said to bring him with her. They needed someone to replace a boy who just left.

A hundred women were inside making clothes, hand sewing for the most part, sitting at tables. A few worked at sewing machines. He was put to work carrying material to the women and in no time he had several admirers who pressed love notes into his hands or blew him kisses when he visited their work stations. There were furs in endless variety and skins of a dozen reptiles. He kept watching for the blue-gray hide and never saw it. He attracted the attention of a gray-haired bookkeeper; she kept smiling at him; "Mexicano", she called him. He tried to talk to her and she spoke Spanish and became very friendly and talkative. He said he knew a little English from school in Mexico and could type and use a computer. A few days later she put him in shipping and receiving, which had a computer. He unpacked a delivery of reptile hides the next week from Real Accessorias. Royal. The hides made him think of the purse though they were inferior and he asked what Real did. She said they made the most expensive purses in the world and outsourced some of their work to Four X's. These hides were nothing special. Real's address was five minutes away. He took a cab to it- a nondescript warehouse half as big as Four X's

Later that night he went to a computer café and downloaded Real. It sold a vast array of purses on line but none of them were priced over eight hundred dollars. He dressed in Armani and went to a boutique that handled the Real line and asked to see the best purses in the store. The clerk showed him well-known designer purses from Italy. What about Real purses. The most expensive the store had were just over a thousand dollars. Perhaps Real was a front and also dealt in legal goods.

He considered looking for a job at Real but thought better of it. Maybe he could hack into their computer and find out what he need to know. He left Four X's and went looking for a computer geek, a peerless hacker. He made friends in a Net Café and soon found one. For a couple hundred he took Carlos to his apartment which looked like the brain center for a start-up. Viewer units against the wall, banks of computers, manuals in heaps, parts and papers everywhere. The guy began hacking away and after five hours said it was impossible-their system was as hacker-proof as the Pentagon. Carlos tried a second hacker a few days later with the same result. The hacker said he could work on it for a year and doubted that he would be successful.

He would have to go to Real seeking work. He decided to go in his Armani seeking employment as a manufacturer's rep.

He said he was from Argentina but he could get by in Portuguese and would work on a "commission only" basis, developing new accounts for Real. He believed in their line and knew he could represent it successfully. The sales manager was so impressed by Carlos that he took an interest in him and decided to develop him. He was a fifty year old man who thought he saw himself in Carlos; he knew women would like him. On the third day he introduced him to the staff, from the girls sewing and gluing, to the cutters, to the shipping clerks and the front office- the bookkeepers and the financial officer. He noted a room with computers against a wall and two women working. One was twenty six, pretty, and looked like a model for eyeglasses. She was the one who he would start seeing as soon as people got used to him. This didn't take any time at all. He made a big hit with them and no one thought it strange when he started talking to her everyday. No one noticed her give him her cell number.

In days he had a date with her to go dancing. She was a divorcee with a four year degree in accounting. He took her to a reggae club. He got her a little drunk on Rum drinks and danced close to her to The First is the Deepest and felt her melting. She didn't want to be picked up at her apartment and didn't say why; he assumed she had a child.

She was very pale and slender, a lovely girl with lustrous chestnut hair. She got very excited when he held her in the dance close and sat talking excitedly at their table afterwards. You're so much fun, she said. I can't believe you've never been with a girl.

I lived at home with my mother. I'm only seventeen.

He wasn't taking any chances; said he was very attracted to girls but he had always been too shy for a serious relationship.

His plan was simple. He wanted her to fall in love with him and lead him to them-the poachers. He realized he wasn't just doing it for Joan anymore. When he saw the reptile hides at Four X's he realized that they were destroying whole species and he wanted to do something to help. He had moved back into a luxury hotel on the beach. She knew he was working on a commission basis and thought his money must have been inherited. She was dying of curiosity and asked to see his place. He took her to his hotel and she took his hand in the elevator and smiled at him prettily.

This is so expensive, she said. Why don't you have your own place?

I will.

I want to help you find it.

Alright.

He carried her inside and took her to the bed, then left her to get champagne. He popped it and poured two flutes. They sat side by side on the bed and he proposed a toast.

To us, he said.

You have such a way, she said. It's so hard to believe you haven't been with a girl.

I haven't.

But why me?

You're just my type.

You think?

Yes. I've waited until I was sure it was right.

And that's me?

That's what I felt when I first met you at Real. I felt that you were the one.

That's so …..lovely. And you're such a gentleman. You would never do anything.

I think we should get to know each other, he said. And a guy can't show too much respect.

Yes…..lovely…. I'll have more champagne. So you're serious about me?

As I said. I knew from the first minute .

Sort of like love at first sight?

It's too soon to tell but it feels really wonderful . I kinda feel it all over.

You get very excited.

I do by you. I never did before.

Yes, so you think you really like me?

How could any guy not like you? You're beautiful.

I'll have some more champagne. Just a little. So where do you want to take me? I mean on our next date.

To the beach.

Alright. Do you want me to go topless?

I think I'd be embarrassed.

So you really don't know what to do. I mean with a girl?

I'll probably figure it out once I get started.

Well, you have to start by kissing the girl.

On the first date?

I think we can kiss on the first date.

He took her glasses off and kissed her and she threw her arms around him and pushed him back and kept kissing him. In a matter of seconds she was out of her clothes and pulling his off.

He spent forever giving her foreplay, kissing her, grazing on her, and then rode her until he had squeezed the last orgasm out of her.

That was so wonderful, he said. I never dreamt it could be like that. Wow! We gotta do that all the time.

Did I do it right? You sort of turned something loose, like, you know, the animal in me. Wow! It was there all along and I didn't know it.

Chapter Fifteen

She thought she had won the lottery of love. He took her to a posh night club the next night and told her he loved her. She believed it and wanted to tell him about her child but was afraid. After dinner and dancing and a bottle of champagne he started talking about how he wanted them to grow with the company together. She said she wanted it too and thought he was going to make a wonderful representative for Real. She was sure he was going to get them more accounts. He said he wanted her to teach him everything about the business but it might not be that easy because they were very secretive about a lot of things.

It must be because they don't want their competitor's wise to new items, he suggested.

That's part of it, but there are other things.

Really?

I love my job and they pay me really good.

I understand but if it's important for me to know, I mean, to do my job better.

I agree. If you're going to be with us you should know what you're getting yourself into. I suppose you'll find out sooner or later. It's really impossible to keep something like this secret. With all the product out there. Everyone wants it. Not everyone. The Super Rich. And they're the big flaunters. That's what they're into. Flaunting.

You must be talking about illegal things.

Sure. You know what I mean.

So they have factories.

Yes. Just down the street. It's a much smaller operation than ours, but it makes more profit than ours does. Much more.

Is it true that women will pay ten thousand dollars for one purse?

Oh, many times that. It's these people who have so many millions.

Where does it all come from?

Paraguas. It's a couple hundred miles from here in the Amazon. Is it a City?

It's a town. Real has a trading post there on a river. The natives bring furs and hides from up and down the river.

Will they ask me to sell these things?

In time. I'm sure they will, yes.

Real can't be the only one that's doing this.

Oh, no but we dominate in some luxury items, like purses and belts. Almost all of these items are made just down the street.

Will I ever get to see it?

I could take you there tonight if you want to see. There are a couple people working. If they see me with you they won't think anything about it.

I'd love to see it.

We can stop by on the way back. Oh, by the way I've got bad news about something. It's that time of the month.

He didn't believe it. She needed the night off to recover.

Chapter Sixteen

They had the cab wait while they went into a small two-story building. There were a few women working at benches. She showed him a trove of illicit coats, shoes, and accessories. He saw a belt like Sue's but no purses. He asked about purses.

Yes, the purses. That's what we're all about, she said. We send them all over the world. Usually the women carry them to the United States and Saudi Arabia. Everywhere. They're not inspected that way and no one pays attention.

Hundreds of purses?

Thousands.

And you've got women carrying them on planes?

Yes. It's a very big operation. We had a woman who managed them for us and moved the money and dealt with our outlets in Milan and Rome and Paris. She was so wonderful. I loved her. She was just a girl but a sort of genius at management. Everyone loved her and she sure knew how to deal with men. Carlos thought of how Maxwell had praised her inner quality. Then she died and now it's not the same. Now Jorge tries to manage everything over the phone. It's a mess. Gertrude and I have to deal with it and it doesn't flow anymore.

So what happened to her?

I don't know; she just disappeared.

You must have some idea, said Carlos.

Her face clouded.

It was like total chaos here for months. There was talk of the police, that she might have talked to the police. They were on her trail- I think in Italy.

Did Real think she was stealing?

No. No one accused her of stealing. I would be the first to know that, but the books balanced.

She must have been local.

No. She lived in Florida. Her name was Joana. But you asked about the purses. I'll see if security will let us in.

No. Don't.

I've got a better idea, let's go to shipping.

She took him to the shipping room and found a couple purses in boxes. One looked like Joan's.

Chapter Seventeen

Carlos told his boss a couple days later that his uncle had died in Mexico City. He'd be back in a week. He took a private plane to Boas, which had the closest airstrip to Paraguas but was still almost fifty miles down-river. Carlos found himself in the heart of the rain forest. He called Gutierez and told him where he was. He had solved the mystery of his wife's death. Now he was going to make a case against Real and shut down the whole operation. He told him everything he had discovered. Gutierez told him to get back to Mexico, he was going to get himself killed, that it was none of his concern. He couldn't change the world. Come back to Rio. He would send someone to get him. He told him where to stay.

Carlos wanted to tie up some loose ends; he wanted to go to the authorities with the evidence necessary to shut down the entire operation. In Boas he asked how he could get to Paraguas and was told that he could reach it by boat in a day. One left the next morning. Carlos thought of renting a boat and leaving that night, but decided to go as a peasant so as not to attract attention. He bought some used clothes and a ratty satchel, a sort of carpet bag. In it he put his cell phone and a few changes of underwear. He kept his money in a money belt. He spent the rest of the day in a bar practicing Portuguese.

The next day the river ride wound through a jungle of trees-millions of trees. He enjoyed standing on the deck and watching the shore for wildlife. Birds in endless variety perched on fallen trees and floated overhead. The river snaked into a canopied rainforest that blocked out the sun in stretches. Villages appeared at intervals with naked Indians and scampering children who waved back to him. He was struck by the overwhelming strangeness of the world, its smells and sounds as much as it's sights. He slept fitfully and woke at first light to resume his post on the boat's deck. He saw Brazilian cormorants on the shore scoot into the water in unison and the outline of a village behind trees and people running.

The boat docked and the natives brought fresh fruits which they sold to the cook. Children and women stared at him, open-mouthed. He did not think the girls, naked save for their loin cloths, were pretty. They seemed short, strange and savage. Then the boat was moving away from the shore, blowing its whistle. He waved to the children and threw them coins. The crew served them fruit cut up on a charger and it tasted to him like paradise. Around six that night they arrived in Paraguas.

The next morning he found the trading post on the river and visited it for an hour. The trader was talkative and said he was filling in for the owner, Toledo, who was in Rio. Carlos saw no signs of any wild animal products but felt that it must do more than sell sundries because its stock was paltry and no one came in for a half hour. He told the clerk his Portuguese was bad because he was from Mexico and that he needed work. The trader gave him an address in town where he could rent a room and told him to contact Gonzalez at the bar there. He would give him work.

Doing what? he asked.

Trapping, he said.

The bar was alfresco in a street of slummy stores. Gonzalez was not there but came two hours later with another young man. Chino- "Chinaman" in Spanish. They were both drunk. Carlos told him what he wanted and the two said they were happy to meet a Mexican. They weren't going trapping. They had just come back and were busy spending money they had made. They had been drinking for three days. They were going into the rain forest to fuck Chingas. Did he want to come?

He said sure, but he was broke.

They laughed and said you didn't need money to fuck Chingas. Not much. And they were flush because they had just trapped a McLean's Macaw.

It's terrible the fuck job they give us, said Gonzalez. I read in a magazine from the States that people have paid ten thousand dollars for one bird.

Chino and I have trapped three and got 50 dollars a piece for them.

A half of percent, said Carlos.

Educated, said Gonzalez. You count good. It's a terrible fuck job.

Ask for more, said Carlos

No one else deals in these things, said Gonzalez. Only Toledo.

I think he would give us more if we demanded, said Chino.

So what else will we trap? asked Carlos.

Whatever they ask for, said Gonzalez.

I think the giant lizards, said Chino.

If there are any to trap, said Gonzalez. We take too many. I tell them not so many. You gotta let them come back.

Shit, we haven't checked the traps for cats! said Chino. Not for over a week. If we have a cat it's starved by now.

There are no more cats, said Gonzalez.

There could be. Sometimes you are surprised, said Chino.

Let's go, said Carlos. I'd love to see.

What? Empty traps?

But Gonzalez, there could be a cat. And then we would be rich.

What kind of cat, asked Carlos.

Probably a jaguar.

Sometimes it is something else in the traps for the cats, said Gonzalez, the pessimist.

Carlos drank sparingly. When they finally wandered down to the river it was dark. They decided to try to find the cat traps anyway. They set off and docked an hour later where they had marked a tree but it was an old marking and there was no trap there. Chino got bit by an insect and wanted to go back to Paraguas. Gonzalez still wanted to fuck Chingas but after a lengthy altercation he agreed to return to Paraguas. On the way back they met someone they knew, a young man who sometimes trapped with them. He invited them to a poker game in Paraguas. Carlos ended up in a bar with five men playing poker. He had only played poker a few times but they were so drunk Carlos was able to play competitively and actually found himself up a few reals after a couple hours.

What do you think of Bin Laden, asked Gonzalez. We

all love him for fucking the United States. What do you think, will they catch him?

How could I know this? asked Carlos. I'm just a dumb Mexican.

You've come to a good place to make money but we must figure out a way to get our animals to Rio, said Gonzalez. All of the trappers would have to get together.

You need a representative to go there for you and find a buyer and take the product there yourself, said Carlos.

He's right, of course, said Gonzalez. But it would be impossible to organize these brigands. They take advantage of us because we are stupid and uneducated. I was a fisherman. Most of us were nothing.

I worked for a shoemaker, said Chino.

I think the boys would go along, said a third drunk. Maybe we should send the Mexican.

I am only a dumb Mexican, said Carlos.

They played cards and drank aquadiente until they could stay awake no longer and staggered off to their beds.

The next afternoon Carlos found his new friends, three this time.

Preguntas is dead, said Chino. He played cards with us last night.

From drink? asked Carlos.

No. Someone was waiting for him at his house. He owed the man money and man shot him.

Good, said Chino. Preguntas was a piece of shit.

He always asked questions, commented Carlos. That's why they called him Preguntas?

Yes, said Chino. And he never paid back. So it's no great loss.

I remember, said Carlos. He was the one who wanted me to represent you in Rio.

I have no memory of this, said Chino.

You don't? asked Gonzalez,

No. From the drink.

He wanted me to represent all the trappers and get a better deal, said Carlos.

Yes, I remember, said Gonzalez.

Everyone would have to agree, said Carlos. Then if we got better deal from a new buyer in Rio we could deal with Toledo here.

We all know each other, said Gonzalez. I could talk to the poachers. We should find them all to fuck Chingas with us. We can't fuck them all ourselves. There are far too many.

How do you do this? asked Carlos. Don't the men of the tribe object?

They don't know.

I think we should check the cats, said Chino.

There are no fucking cats, Chino, said Gonzalez. There hasn't been a cat in months.

I have a feeling, said Chino. The beautiful thing about this work is that you are flat broke. You are dead. And then you wake up a rich man because there's big money waiting for you in the jungle. Like a cat. It could be there.

There are no fucking cats, Chino, said Gonzalez.

We could take the boat, check for cats then go another couple kilometers to Colos and look up Pocito and Jorge The will know where Contras is. Then we can borrow Contra's boat and go up river fast to Torrelinqua and visit the Chingas.

I have too much of a hangover to fuck Chingas, said Gonzalez.

You will feel better by then. The air on the river will be good for you. I have a headache too from last night. I lost all my money. We need a score bad. I say we check the cats.

There are no fucking cats.

Yesterday we were too drunk to find the traps, said Carlos. Now I bet we could find them.

Alright, to shut Chino up I agree, said Gonzalez and they set off.

They ran out of gas halfway to the traps and had to row and it was again dark when they found a marking. This time it was the right one and they found a trap a half an hour later with a large dead snake in it.

Is it worth anything, asked Carlos?

Not worth a shit, said Chino.

They found a second and a third trap and they were both empty.

Chino said there was a fourth trap but Gonzalez said he was loco, there were only three traps and they had to get back to the river to bum some gas from a boat or they would never get back to Paraguas. They were too far to row. They met a friend on the river a half hour later but he didn't have enough gas for himself. He gave them a tow to a village where they could buy gas. Carlos had to pay for the four liters of gas because the others were broke from the card game. They proceeded on to Colos but no one was there. Someone said the three men who gave them a tow were trapping lizards.

What kind? asked Carlos.

Giant ones. Good luck to them, said Chino. They won't find shit.

Gonzalez said they should go to a bar where the trappers would come when they got back from checking their traps. They waited a couple hours until Contras showed up alone carrying a burlap sack. He had a lizard in the sack. Carlos asked to see it.

That's not so easy, said Contras.

They spent a minute getting it out. It tried to bite and escape and put up a game fight.

A magnifico, Contras said. Carlos recognized the blue-gray skin. Its eyes seemed to bug out and its blue and pink tongue darted.

He thought of how beautiful and perfect it was compared to the trappers. They made him think of three young derelicts.

How can you fuck Cingas when you are penniless, said Contras. Don't ask me for a loan. You already owe me.

We are good for it, said Chino.

In a year. No. I have no interest in this. Now, when you get money, it's a different story; there is a new tribe. I saw them yesterday. They just moved into the area. They are nomads. Very nice people and the women are better than the Cingas we are used to.

I want to see them, said Chino.

We need a score, said Gonzalez.

What will you get for the giant? asked Chino.

A hundred dollars.

So much?

I will demand it

He might give you fifty dollars, said Gonzalez. We have decided to form a group and demand more.

Like a union, said Chino.

You are dreaming, said Contras.

Chapter Eighteen

They returned to Paraguas empty handed a couple hours later and decided to trap birds. This was hard work but they were desperate men. They planned to set out early in the morning but ended up rendezvousing at the bar at noon. They began drinking on Carlos at the bar. An hour later a friend joined them and gave them the good news. Loco had found a herd of rare peccaries three hours up river. Carlos asked what they were and learned they were related to pigs. Loco needed all the men he could get. There could be a hundred peccaries. Chino said they would all be rich if it were true. And well fed because they were good eating. The four men talked about going up river to hunt peccaries for an hour. Everyone but Carlos was drunk. Then they got in the boat and headed for the village where Loco was waiting for them.

Why doesn't he use natives? asked Carlos.

They would kill him and take his hides, said Chino.

Besides, you can't give them shotguns. They won't give them back. They run away with them.

A couple hours later Carlos recognized markings on the tree for the cats and said he wanted to check the traps. He would run and it would only take him minutes. They docked and he ran through the undergrowth to the first trap. It had a rodent in it. He released it. In the second, he found an exotic cat that made him think of the belt and the jacket. It was not a jaguar. He wondered what they were calling a jaguar. He photographed it with his cellphone and released it and went to the next trap, which was empty.

I told you there were no fucking cats, said Gonzalez when Carlos returned to the boat.

An hour later they arrived at the village. Loco was in a hut with three trappers drinking aquadiente. He was glad to see them. They had shotguns and plenty of shells for the peccaries.

Here is the Mexicano, said Gonzalez. He will be our salvation.

This is what we need, said Loco. All the trappers know. We are talking about sending him to Rio to find another buyer. We will get fifty dollars for a peccary from Toledo. It's an insult. One hide can make three or four shoes and I know as a fact they bring one thousand dollars in Rio. No one knows about New York or Paris or London. I'm sure much more.

How many peccaries are there? asked Carlos.

No one knows, said Loco. We don't go far enough into the jungle. If we get lucky I am going to take a group deep into the jungle. I will be able to pay for food and more ammo.

But in this herd, how many? asked Chino.

Oh, we struck gold. This herd could have over a hundred. I saw dozens.

Where are they? asked Chino.

Maybe a kilometer, said Contras.

Or gone, said Gonzalez. I've hunted the little fuckers. They don't stay in one place.

They managed to get on their way around eleven o'clock the next morning. Carlos saw Macaws and dozens of birds, mammals, and reptiles. He remembered reading that most of the terrestrial species lived in the rain forests. An hour later they found peccaries in the jungle near a large patch of land that farmers had cleared through slashing and burning. Loco suggested that three of the men drive game into it and three wait for the peccaries to run into the clearing where it would be easy to shoot them. Carlos volunteered to act as a driver. He and Loco and a third man made a wide arc then began marching on the clearing banging on pans and shouting. Hundreds of feet from the clearing they heard the shotguns going off and Loco called to Carlos to run. When they reached the clearing they saw pigs running in the distance. The shotguns were still firing. Carlos heard a rustle in the undergrowth and squealing and saw a sow with her piglets run into the clearing and held his fire.

Don't shoot! She has young. Think of tomorrow. Loco shot obliquely and the sow dropped on its side and its piglets rioted, squealing noisily around it. Carlos wanted to kill Loco and all the others but knew he had to get the goods on them and turn them in. He was so tender-hearted he actually began crying at the sight of the convulsing sow. Now Loco was running, chasing a boar that had broken into the clearing. The shotgun tore up clods of dirt but the boar disappeared into the sedge. A few desultory shots rang out and the men began gathering to collect the carcasses. They were rich men. But Loco's appetite was not sated. He felt that the surviving peccaries would have stopped in the jungle a few kilometers away. He proposed that they dig a trench across the clearing just beyond the jungle. They had brought three shovels and dug this trench two hundred feet long in a couple hours. The oxidized red earth dug easily. Then they set off and in a couple hours saw a pig's rump as shades of evening began falling. They cut a wide arc around the sighting, spread out over a half mile, and began driving the animals with one man flanking them on each side, walking ahead. An hour later the peccaries began emerging into the clearing and spilling into the trench. Many fortuitously avoided the trench but twenty-three peccaries were trapped and clubbed to death with shovels. Carlos had to join in the slaughter and suffered deeply for the animals; the wretched cacophony of men laughing and shouting curses and animals squealing seemed to last forever.

The six built a fire and sat around it drinking aquadiente. They had brought three bottles, enough to get drunk; Carlos took an occasional sip. Then they began discussing the shares. Gonzalez assumed the shares would be equal. Chino agreed.

Fuck your mother! said Loco. You work for me. I promised you equal shares but I keep half. It has always been this way when I take out an expedition.

Yes, but this is no such thing, said Gonzalez.

The altercation degenerated into curses. Gonzalez then drew his pistol and shot Loco in the leg and Loco shot Gonzalez dead. One of Loco's men knocked Chino insensate with a shovel. Carlos dashed into the jungle.

Don't kill the Mexicano! cried Loco, holding his leg. We need help with all these pigs.

Two men followed Carlos into the jungle and pleaded with him to return. He was afraid they would kill him at first but they explained that they knew he had no loyalty to Gonzalez or Chino.

He had just come from Mexico. They wanted him to join forces with him and have his share. They made sense and he did not think he could find his way back alone.

Agreed, he said. The share is fair. I have no objection to it. When he came near the fire he noticed the two bodies were gone. Loco had kicked them into the trench with his good leg.

Chino was still alive, said Loco. But now he will die with his brothers, the pigs.

No, said Carlos. Chino had nothing to do with it. We must save him. He looked for him in the trench and found him, but he was dead.

Chapter Nineteen

Loco's wound was not a flesh wound; it continued to hemorrhage and Loco died before first light. Succio, Torres, and Carlos buried the three in the trench. Carlos assured Succio and Torres that he didn't want a share; they could have his share. He really didn't deserve it. They wouldn't hear of this and said they wanted Carlos to lead them. They wanted Carlos to negotiate a better deal for them; they had heard how he had come to save all the trappers. He was educado and well-spoken. Many of them were calling him "El Salvador." He protested that he was just Mexicano and no one should call him anything else. They now had thirty-five hides. Skinning all the hogs took them all of two days. Then they returned to the river and found their boat where they had hidden it and set off for Paraguas. At the first village they delivered the piglets into the safekeeping of the Indians.

They arrived in Paraguas just before the trading post closed and Carlos demanded ten thousand dollars for the hides and left when the trader laughed at him. Carlos said he would fly them to Rio. The trader caught up with him just before they boarded and wanted to see the hides. He said that if Carlos would not disclose the transaction he would pay the money and take thirty-five more. The deal was done and Carlos told his men about the agreement. The next day a dozen men came to the bar where they were drinking and hailed Carlos "El Salvador" and said they wanted to hunt peccaries with him. They wanted to catch all those that had escaped. They wanted Carlos to have half the profit and they would share the rest. They believed they would still earn much more than they had ever earned. Carlos said they would all take equal shares. He bought a case of aquadiente and they drank themselves into a stupor. The men insisted that they were not going to hunt until they celebrated their new agreement by fucking Chingas. Someone had been talking to the Chingas and a multitude would come to drink aquadiente and fuck for beads and trinkets. They knew what the Chingas liked. Shiny things. Carlos thought of his wife's jewelry. They also wanted kitchen utensils and anything with Mickey Mouse or Donald Duck on it.

They were supposed to set out the next night and planned to rendezvous at the bar at six o'clock and meet the Chingas an hour's trek into the jungle, but they started playing poker, and were still playing the next morning. They didn't wake up until noon. No one felt like it so they waited a couple days until everyone could get up before noon. Then twenty set out around six and arrived at the site where the Chingas women went for water, a spring, but none were there. They waited around an hour debating whether they should look for them or try again the next day. Carlos hoped that the Chingas had left the area but was assured that it wouldn't happen for months. The Chingas were harvesting Casava they had planted while their men hunted monkeys with poison darts. Carlos asked if they ever killed Brazilians or Whites or whatever they called people like Carlos. They said hardly ever. The men decided to go looking for them and found an encampment that had been recently abandoned. So the Chingas are gone, said Carlos, relieved. They can't have gone far, the men said. Someone was sure they had gone east for some reason and struck off in that direction. In a couple hours they made a camp and built a bonfire and began drinking the white firewater. The jungle sounds were unusually loud and Carlos had a sense of foreboding. He tried to persuade the men to give up their insane quest for Chingas but they were too drunk to listen to reason. They all woke by noon and began marching through the jungle. Someone saw a jaguar and they got very excited and began building traps. They shot a large rodent which they used as bait. They played cards and drank for a couple days, then lost interest in trapping and decided to look for Chingas again. The next day they saw two bathing in a stream. They made Carlos think of a tableau from Gauguin. They smiled and seemed friendly. One of the men talked Chingas. Carlos was sure he heard "Mickey Mouse". An arrangement was made to meet with them and their friends that night. Carlos thought they were prettier than the girls he had seen on the river. They felt no shame about their nakedness. Carlos wondered how old they were and asked one of the men who said no one knew. The girls didn't know. They only had a couple hundred words in their language. There was a word for one, two, three but after that everything was "many."

The men went back to their camp and returned at dark to the spring but the Chingas never showed. Carlos remembered being stood up by a girl in high school.

Now we can go back, said Carlos.

Maybe the traps will have a cat. That would pay for the expedition.

The men were sure that the Chingas would come at nightfall the next night. Carlos should be happy. At last they were going to fuck Chingas.

The next night Carlos suggested that he stay and guard the camp. The men wouldn't let him. They said no one would find the camp and he was going to really like it. It was something everyone needed to try. They set out for the spring and wonder of wonders a dozen or so Chingas women were there. They had built a small fire. They started talking to the men and drinking firewater with them and after an hour pairs began breaking off and going into the bush for love. Carlos saw brown buttocks rising through the tall grass. One of the men explained that that was how Chingas did it. They were primitivos. If you put them on their backs they would cover their faces and laugh like fools. He heard some feminine laughter and wondered if this was what was going on. Then reinforcements showed up- a dozen more girls. He wondered if they had finished doing the dishes or some analogous domestic chore. Two pretty sisters sat down on each side of him and started talking Chingas. He was sure he heard one of them say Mickey Mouse. They wanted to drink and made him join them and then they were pulling his clothes off and he saw a pair of bottoms flicker in the fire light and thought he heard the jungle noises getting louder. He wanted to see if the girl would laugh so he put her on her back and she laughed hilariously but didn't cover her face. And then the other girl began crying Chingas! Chingas!, which he realized meant fuck in their language. That's why they called the tribe that. He didn't know what to do. He didn't want to have sex without a condom but the other girl heard him say condom and produced one. He was putting it on when he heard a whoosh and a scream and voice cry "spears"! He scrambled to his feet and ran into the jungle naked and heard screams and saw men running in all directions-naked men and women.

He recalled the approximate location of the camp and sprinted through the noisy jungle. He could hear shots and screams all the way back. It didn't take him fifteen minutes. His feet and legs were torn up but he was relieved to be alive and unharmed. Then his men began appearing. Eight made it, some injured, two badly. They said the Chingas had killed the rest and impaled them on trees with their spears.

Did they always impale men they caught with their wives? asked Carlos.

Yes, that was their custom.

What about the women?

They would just beat the women.

Carlos asked if they still wanted to fuck Chingas.

They said no, not those anyway. He wondered how many poachers lived a normal life expectancy.

The men got back to Paraguas a couple days later, sadder but wiser. He heard a couple men say it was too bad about the dead but it was good for poaching. The fewer poachers the better because there wasn't enough game. When were they going to hunt peccaries? Carlos said he had to make a trip to Boas first and left on the river, planning to fly from Boas to Rios on the next plane.

Chapter Twenty

The day he arrived in Rios he moved into a hotel on the beach near his old one and took a couple days to gather his thoughts and prepare his case against Real and its jungle outpost. He hoped to shut down its operation in South America, which would lead to an investigation of its Tampa connection. He had planned to bring the poachers into his dragnet but now saw this as futile. He realized that there was an inexhaustible supply of poachers and arresting the survivors of the Chingas attack would accomplish nothing.-others would soon take their place. He had photos of animals and hides, photos of Real's auxiliary factory and trading post.

He went to a barber and got a haircut and went to the Palace of Justice the next morning looking like new money. When he told a receptionist why he was there she ushered him into the office of a minor official. This polite young man discussed the matter briefly and left: he returned a hour later and escorted him to office of an undersecretary, with flags, portraits and a big mahogany conference table. Men in military uniforms came in and introduced themselves-generals and ministers. They wanted to know everything-to debrief Carlos. They spent the morning talking to him. Then the young man asked him to return to the small office and assured him that action would be taken. He asked Carlos if he would be returning to his hotel and spoke with him about Brazil and his family for an hour before thanking him profusely and telling him that Brazil thanked him for his service.

Carlos was returning to his hotel in a cab when he saw a helicopter drop and hover above an intersection one block ahead. What was it doing? Then he remembered McMahon. He threw the door open and rolled out. As soon as he was able, he stood up and began running. He heard a crash but didn't look back, darted between buildings, found an alley; worked his way through a maze of buildings and streets until he found a cab parked at a curb and jumped in.

Where to? the driver asked.

The nearest barber.

He had his beard shaved and bought shades at a sundries across the street. Now he had to get his papers out of the hotel. He went to it, saw no-one in the hall, got in and out of his room and away. Of course he could not use his papers at the airport. He called Gutierez from a payphone and told him what had happened. Gutierez had him stay on the phone, called Hugo and set up a rendezvous minutes later.

Hugo met him at a tony bar with music and dancers. He sat smiling at Carlos, waiting for Carlos to talk.

I think I know why you're smiling, said Carlos.

I'm happy you're alive.

You were right. I wasn't ready. I was an idiot.

Not an idiot. You lacked sophistication in the ways of the world. You thought you could fight the world.

I did what I could.

You could keep trying until you got yourself killed.

No thanks. I've had enough.

I would hope so.

But how are you going to get me out of Brazil?

Hugo opened his briefcase and took out a new passport. You are now Edwardo Lopez, a Mexican citizen. We will be leaving in a couple days on a private jet from a small airstrip about one hundred kilometers out of Rio. I don't think they'll be looking there. It's used mostly by drug dealers and smugglers. That would be out of character for you.

Why in two days? asked Carlos.

We can't miss Carnival.

Carlos remembered the activities in the streets. The city was alive, even the café had an unusual aspect-people were freer, louder, drinking more.

So you thought you would save the animals and find the people who killed your wife.

Yes

So, now you have found them. You see government is God. No one is above it and the media is its agent. So why did they kill her?

The Europeans were after her. The Italian police. They were probably afraid she'd talk. That's only speculation, but we don't know anything for certain. Real could have tried to kill me today. But I don't think I'll go back to the Brazilian police and tell them.

I wouldn't, said Hugo.

And what about the money?

My uncle is recovering more of it.

I will never know how she got the money. She may have been collecting more than she was reporting to Real or she may have met billionaires who were giving it to her. She was a courtesan. Or it may have been a combination of both. That wouldn't surprise me.

Do you still love her?

More than ever. I was like her child. She lived for me.

So what will you do now that she's gone and you've learned that you can't fight them?

You mean today? I can't fight here but there will be other opportunities. I love the animals. I intend to use Joan's money to fight for them.

Chapter Twenty One

The next night the two watched the carnival from the terrace of a café. Waves of dancers in monochromatic blocks swept by –blue, pink, white, yellow. Samba music, laughter, voices. Then he saw her. He was sure it was Joan and ran into a crowd of female dancers after her. Hugo was soon beside him.

What are you doing? he asked.

She's here. I saw her. My wife.

Alright. Good. Let's find her.

They were swept along in a crowd of dancing bodies. They found themselves in a sea of red feathers. The music and confusion entranced him-the fever of excitement and carnality. Girls kissed him and gave him drinks out of flasks, exotic flavors mixed with kisses. Hugo was kissing all the girls, kissing and squeezing. And then Carlos saw her- Joan's double- a striking beauty who looked like she was dressed only in red feathers. She smiled into his eyes, shaking all over. She was a little drunk and thought he was the most handsome young man she'd ever seen.

Joan, it's you, he said holding her hands. I knew you would be here. That's why I came.

I'm glad you came, belo. What is your name?

Carlos.

Yes, of course. I've been waiting for you too. And what did you call me, Carlos?

Joan, I knew you were alive and waiting for me here. Can I kiss you?

I wish you would.